DOCTO

'I never want to see you again,' Fiona Meredith told Dr Stephen Radcliffe eleven years ago. But she never told him the real, tragic, reason for her action. And neither imagined they would ever meet again . . .

Helen Upshall lives in Bournemouth with her husband, now retired. When quite young she became interested in Doctor Nurse stories, reading her much older sister's magazine serials instead of getting on with the dusting, so it was a natural progression to go into nursing in the late 1940s. Since she took up writing, ideas have come from a variety of sources—personal experiences of relatives and friends, and documentaries on television.

Doctor From the Past is Helen Upshall's eighth Doctor Nurse Romance.

DOCTOR FROM
THE PAST

BY

HELEN UPSHALL

MILLS & BOON LIMITED
15–16 BROOK'S MEWS
LONDON W1A 1DR

First published in Great Britain 1986
by Mills & Boon Limited

© Helen Upshall 1986

Australian copyright 1986
Philippine copyright 1986

ISBN 0 263 75562 2

Set in 10 on 11½ pt Linotron Times
03–1186–52,800

Photoset by Rowland Phototypesetting Limited
Bury St Edmunds, Suffolk
Made and printed in Great Britain by
William Collins Sons & Co Ltd, Glasgow

CHAPTER ONE

FIONA sipped her tea, and surveyed the muddle on the living-room floor. Her eyes still felt heavy from the tedious drive home the previous evening. Tameless wind and rain had made it quite a perilous journey, but she was glad that she'd stayed on with the others for coffee and a chat. The course had been efficiently organised, and well worth the journey, but it must have been almost midnight before she fell into bed, leaving her case of belongings and a stack of textbooks and notebooks just where they were now. She rubbed her eyes and cheeks vigorously to try to wake herself up. Her face still tingled from the cold water splash she'd given it ten minutes ago. It was likely to be a long day, she knew. There were the elderly to visit; most of them would have been glad enough to have the assistant health visitor call on them during the past ten days, but Fiona had been doing this same job for nearly six years now. Living in a rural area had its compensations, one of them being that you grew into the community, and her ageing patients were all familiar to her, and she to them. The district she was responsible for took in several widespread villages, with the small market town of Kenelm as the core where the Health Centre to which Fiona was attached was situated.

She poured away the rest of her tea, wishing that she'd made coffee instead, which might have woken her up more quickly. She was on her way to the bathroom when the telephone broke the silence of Forest View Chalet,

5

and she quickly ran back to the living-room and picked up the receiver.

'Fiona Meredith speaking,' she croaked, her voice strange after a night of silence.

'Miss Meredith—Nurse——?' The voice at the other end was faint, but with some encouragement Fiona learned that one of the young mothers in the area had fallen down the stairs while carrying her five-month-old baby.

'Stay right where you are, Anita, and I'll be with you in five minutes,' Fiona ordered.

That was hardly possible considering that Fiona wasn't dressed yet, but she raced into the bedroom, wriggled herself into a pair of dark brown cords, pulled a thick sweater over her head, and picking up her bag opened the door of her mobile home bungalow to face more of the same weather as yesterday.

'Yuk!' was the appropriate description, but there was no one around to hear her, not even Cassie, her twenty-month-old golden retriever who had been farmed out during her absence to James Coudray, one of the partners at the health centre.

The engine of Fiona's blue Morris Ital stalled, but ignited again at the next turn of the key, and while it warmed up Fiona clicked her seat belt into position. Backing out of the small parking space was hazardous, but there wasn't time to sit and wait for the rear windscreen to clear. Fortunately Sixpenny Lane was deserted, and with sprays of mud shooting out from each side of the vehicle she sped off to the far end of the village where Anita lived on a housing estate.

Presumably Anita's husband had already left for work because there was no car in the driveway, so Fiona drove straight up into the car-port. She found the front door unlocked, and inside the tiny hallway sat Anita at the foot of the stairs, cradling her baby in her arms.

'Oh, Fiona, I'm so glad you're here,' she sobbed. 'I didn't know what to do.'

'How did you manage to telephone?' Fiona asked.

'I hopped to the kitchen, but my ankle is so painful I couldn't get any farther. I thought it best to stay put with the baby. Look at her first, Fiona—is she all right? Keith will kill me if she's hurt.'

Fiona picked up the baby girl, who responded with an easy, toothless smile. 'She looks fine to me. How far did you fall?'

'Only three steps, thank goodness, but I twisted my ankle as I reached the bottom. Look, it's terribly swollen.'

Fiona took the baby into the lounge and laid her in the carrycot which she knew was always on the settee.

'Now,' she said to Anita, who was white-faced and trembling from shock. 'Let's get you up on your good leg—that's right—now put your arm round my neck and we should be able to make it to the lounge.' They had ventured a step or two when the doorbell chimed its musical tune.

'That'll be——' Anita began breathlessly.

'Come in—it's not locked,' Fiona called over her shoulder as she urged her patient to hop a few more steps.

'Here—let me.' A strong man was just what was required, but Fiona hadn't anticipated the shock of seeing a familiar face. Anita was swept up into powerful arms and carried to an easy chair.

'Oh, Doctor, thanks for coming,' Anita breathed on a rush of gratitude.

Fiona felt as if she was the one who had taken a

tumble. A tumble back in time. She hadn't heard that voice for eleven years, much less seen the owner of it, but it was as dear to her now as it had ever been.

'What happened?' the doctor asked as he examined Anita's ankle, 'and who are you?' He turned to confront Fiona. *'Good God!'* His voice was harsh, and he looked as stunned as Fiona felt.

'She's our health visitor,' Anita explained. 'Fiona Meredith. I called the health centre first, they said Fiona was back so I rang her, but I didn't know they'd booked a house call as well.'

'Stephen Radcliffe, Mrs——?' he introduced, turning back to Anita, playing for time.

'Boughton, Doctor,' Anita filled in timidly, not understanding the sudden tension which filled the room.

He looked at Fiona again, hardly believing what he saw, and there was a long pause while the mists of time rolled back the years to that last fateful meeting. . . .

A clinical hospital room where Fiona had lain for three weeks after the car crash. Stephen Radcliffe, then her fiancé, and houseman at a Bristol hospital where Fiona had just succeeded in passing her State Registered Final Examination, had been driving the car on their return to Bristol after a family party to celebrate her achievement. She had known little that followed immediately afterwards. There were people, and voices, but they had all seemed so far away. She fought back into reality and as she grew stronger she took an interest in her condition, which was much more serious than Stephen's minor cuts and abrasions. The other car had swerved to avoid them, Stephen had manoeuvred his car in the opposite direction, but both cars skidded to a violent impact on Fiona's side. When she learned the truth about her injuries she knew that her crushed pelvis meant a childless marriage, and to Fiona that meant she could never be the kind of wife Stephen would expect. All their hopes and plans had been erased in that cruel impact. For two days she had churned it over in her mind, trying to come to terms with the situation, but in the end there had only been one solution, and when Stephen came to see her at the weekend she had calmly said: 'I never want to see you again.'

Looking at him now, eleven years later, Fiona couldn't comprehend the hurt she had caused him. He had returned many times, only to be told that she was adamant and meant what she said, but only she knew the disappointment that she would have caused if she had gone ahead with a childless marriage, so she forbade anyone to tell Stephen the truth, and now by the hard look in his dark brown eyes she knew that he was still ignorant of the facts, for which she was grateful. He doesn't know, she thought, he never truly understood and he still hates me for jilting him.

'You're the last person in the world I expected to find still in these parts.' If he was trying to hide the shock of this meeting his voice betrayed him. Fate was a cruel tormentor.

He turned back to Anita abruptly. 'Now then, what have you been doing?'

She explained tearfully, and Stephen's smile was warm and full of sympathy. He observed Anita closely as he felt her foot, ankle and leg.

'A nasty sprain, and an unpleasant shock to find yourself on the floor in a heap, but there's no great damage done, my dear,' his smile widened. 'No need for us to send for an ambulance or anything as dramatic, but you'll need to rest it for a few days.'

'Please check the baby, Doctor,' Anita begged,

'I don't care about me, but if I've done anything to
her——'

'Babies are surprisingly resilient,' he cut in, but he
went to the carrycot, and under the guise of playing ran
his skilful fingers round the baby's neck and body.

'Seems unharmed to me,' he assured Anita as he
stretched to his full height, 'but if anything worries you,
let us know. I expect Fiona will keep an eye on you both.
Have you anyone who can give you a hand in the house?'

'I expect my mother will come and help, and I have a
sister who's unemployed. She won't need to be asked
twice to look after Lucy.'

Stephen perched on the arm of Anita's chair. 'Do you
have pain-killers in the house?' he asked as he rested a
consoling hand on her shoulder.

She nodded, and moving her foot, winced with the
pain.

Stephen slowly turned to face Fiona. The effect of the
emotional disturbance was less traumatic now and his
dark eyes held her gaze with shades of memorable
recognition.

'A cup of tea would be nice, Fiona—for all of us, I
think, and a couple of pain-killers for Mrs Boughton? A
crêpe bandage for support until the swelling goes down
will be beneficial, and if you're not happy about it we'll
get it X-rayed, but I don't honestly think that will be
necessary.'

Fiona went to the kitchen and filled an electric kettle,
and while she waited for the water to boil she searched
for cups, saucers, milk, sugar and spoons. These last
went to the floor with a clatter in her confusion. She had
caught sight of herself in the hall mirror and knew what a
sight she looked. Her hair, varying between shades of
thick or thin honey, couldn't be less well-groomed. It

was shortish, which she preferred for convenience in contrast to the long wavy tresses she'd sported in her teens and early twenties. She had a natural clear, pale complexion but even with no make-up on she was aware of the heightened colour the situation had instigated. She was nervously fidgeting with the re-washed spoons in the tea-towel when she heard the kettle's automatic device switch off, so she put two tea-bags in the teapot and poured the water on quickly. Holding her face aside from the steam she caught the sound of a step behind her.

'How have you been, Fiona?' There was genuine interest in the question, yet awkward distance in evidence.

'Fine, thanks—and you?'

Stephen didn't answer at once and at his silence Fiona glanced over her shoulder at him. Always a handsome figure, faultless in his attention to every detail of his appearance, little seemed to have changed until her eyes really noticed his expression. The pain she saw there couldn't possibly have lasted for the whole eleven years which had passed, even if remnants of her anguish had remained just below the surface. No, Stephen's pain was of a more recent injury.

'Physically, no complaints,' he said curtly, and then with a sigh he added, 'emotionally, for the second time in my adult life I'm shattered. My—er—wife died, so now seemed to be the right time to return to England.'

'Oh, Stephen, I'm so dreadfully sorry, I had no idea.'

His half laugh, half snort was delivered with sarcasm.

'You wouldn't—how could you?—when I emigrated I intended it to be for good.'

He was still bitter, he hadn't forgiven her and that opened up all the old wounds. Wounds which had taken

Fiona a longer time to heal, mentally, than his pride, she suspected. It had taken little more than a year for him to forget her enough to find a new love and marry. Within the year following the accident he had emigrated to Australia, and when news of his marriage reached Fiona's parents via Stephen's father who was a consultant at the large county hospital, they assured Fiona it was a case of love on the rebound. Now, seeing the misery reflected in his eyes, she knew for sure that he had taken a second chance at love and been successful. It wasn't easy for her to be unselfish about it, yet in a way it brought some relief to the perplexities of the past eleven years. She was at a loss to know what to say next, so she stirred the tea and poured milk into the cups.

'Still two sugars?' she asked with casual ease.

'I never *ever* took two,' he said gruffly. 'One, please.'

As if he couldn't bear to be in her company a moment longer he returned to the lounge, and when Fiona followed with the tray of tea he was admiring baby Lucy.

Fiona practically scalded her tongue and throat as she swallowed mouthful after mouthful of tea in her haste to get away. Anita told her where she could find a crêpe bandage in the bathroom cabinet, and with a slight tremble in her fingers Fiona bound up her patient's ankle and made it comfortable on a stool, settling Anita beside the baby's carrycot with anything she thought she might require.

'I'll ring in for Patsy to visit you, and on my way to the Centre I'll call in to tell your mum—how's that?' Fiona suggested helpfully.

'Thanks, Fiona. Don't know what I'd do without you.'

Stephen put his cup down and stood up. 'You're attached to the Centre at Kenelm?' he asked.

Fiona nodded as she walked to the door, and Stephen followed.

'Take care, Mrs Boughton,' he said. 'I'm locum at the Centre for a few weeks so Fiona will be able to keep me informed, but don't be afraid to call me if you're worried.'

Under the car-port Fiona flattened herself against her car door.

'You're blocking the entrance so you'd better go first,' she said.

Stephen hesitated. 'I suppose I ought to apologise.'

'What for?' Fiona asked.

'If my coming here will embarrass you. I really never imagined that we'd ever meet again. I presumed you were married to whoever had so much more to offer you than I did, and that you'd moved away. Mother should have warned me.'

'It wasn't quite like that, Stephen—and I didn't ever expect you to return here to work—but, locum you said? You'll be moving on?'

In her effort to sound disinterested she might almost have been urging him to make his stay a short one. Stephen's brow puckered and his eyes appeared savagely dark.

'My parents are happy to have me and the children home again. The house is large enough for us all—no, I have no such plans at present to look elsewhere. It seems quite providential that old Dr Locke has had to give up.'

'I didn't know that,' she responded quickly with a look of astonishment. 'I've been away on a course. He's not been well for the past few years, but there was no mention of his giving up.'

'I'm sorry to have to be the one to tell you, Fiona—he had a stroke and at the moment is still in hospital.'

'So *you've* stepped into his shoes?' Carelessly she voiced her thoughts aloud.

'No! No one of my age could walk in the steps of Dr Locke's experience. He's been a father to decades of Kenelm children.'

Fiona gazed intently at the bunch of keys in her hand. Dr Locke had certainly been a wonderful friend to her, especially at the time she had returned home to live after doing her midwifery course, and through him she had obtained the post of health visitor for the new centre which had been built six years ago.

'He'll be a great loss to the district,' she said solemnly.

'I understand though that Dr Coudray is well qualified to take the senior post.'

'Oh, he is.' Fiona opened her door quickly and strapped herself in.

'No doubt we shall be bumping into each other from time to time,' Stephen said. 'Are you living at home still?'

'No, I have my own place.' She switched on the engine, indicating that she wished to terminate this irrelevant exchange of gossip. Too much had gone before to make formal polite conversation easy.

Stephen was leaning against the car so she was forced to look up at him as she slowly let out the clutch. His expression was one of bewilderment, but with a hint of a smile he nodded and walked ahead of her to his own car, a very smart Rover, chocolate brown in colour, with the latest registration.

Fiona hoped she hadn't betrayed her own feelings. Her love for Stephen had never changed and she was certain never would. It was a love so exclusive, so honest, so tender that when she had been told about her physical condition after the accident she knew she couldn't hold Stephen to their promises, for children, which they both loved, were longed for as a culmination of that love. It wouldn't have been fair to him to continue with the engagement. What did she have to offer? Only herself, and she no longer felt a whole being. She watched him drive away. Tears of love and bitter anguish clouded her vision, and she was glad of the dark car-port where she blew her nose vigorously, and questioned what wrong she could possibly have done to prompt this sudden stab of fate.

Years of unhappiness and bitterness had passed. Yes, she was forced to admit that she had allowed her bitterness to show. The only good thing about the accident had been that it had happened mid-way between home and Bristol so the hospital where she had been taken had honoured her request for details of her condition to be kept confidential, except to her own parents.

'You shouldn't have made such a hasty decision,' her father had told her kindly after she had broken off her engagement to Stephen. 'It's been a shock to your nervous system. Give yourself a chance to come to terms with the situation, lassie, and you'll find nothing has really changed. If you and Stephen really love each other you'll weather this storm together and pick up your lives—maybe a little wiser—and you'll both have a little more compassion to offer to your patients.'

Fiona knew he had meant it to be constructive advice and now she began to wonder if his loving nature and years of general practice in Kenelm hadn't meant that he was much wiser than she'd wanted to believe at the time. What wouldn't she give now to be able to visit her parents and talk things over, but when her father retired at the age of sixty they had moved back up to border country to live in the fine country house he had inherited

in Selkirk. Fiona could have gone too, but she loved her
job and the familiarity of Kenelm and the outlying
villages so she had bought a double unit mobile home
situated on a farm site in the heart of countryside she had
known from her childhood. She supposed there was a
bond too between herself and the area where Stephen
had grown up, and where his parents still lived. They had
tried to hold on to her after the accident, begging her to
continue visiting, but she had found it all too painful,
and when news of Stephen's marriage became public she
had deemed it prudent to sever all connections with
his family, except polite exchanges whenever they
met.

The very fact that Stephen didn't know she was in
Kenelm must indicate that she was never talked about. If
he'd known he probably would have chosen to go elsewhere to work, but now, ironically, they had been
thrown into the same stable. What was Fiona going to
tell James? There was even more irony in the fact that
just when she was on the brink of accepting his persistent
proposals of marriage, Stephen should turn up out of the
blue as if to condemn her to the reminder that she was
not what the average man expected of a wife. Stephen
couldn't and mustn't ever know the truth. Fiona's heart
missed a beat and then thudded loudly against the wall of
her chest as she realised all the connotations of
Stephen's coming to work at Kenelm. James must be
warned and this would mean a much fuller explanation
of past history than she had so far revealed. His affection
for her and continued pursuance had led her finally to
excusing her refusal on the grounds that she could never
ever bear him children, but he had held her close and
seemed genuine when he said: 'Darling, I love you,
worship and adore *you*—and aren't we both a bit ancient

to become parents even if we considered adoption?'

She had chided him then about being a young forty-four-year-old, and at thirty-two wasn't she in her prime? They had laughed together, and she knew James was urging a positive response to his proposal, yet still she hesitated. Now she wondered if her reticence to take the plunge wasn't all being influenced by some power beyond her control.

Perhaps now was the time to accept James' offer. Stephen had only recently been widowed, she supposed, and he said he had children. He would be passing through the great dark gorge of emotional tragedy, similar to all that she had experienced after the accident. At least she could offer him some sympathy, but it might help the situation if he realised from the start that she was about to become James Coudray's wife.

As she drove home Fiona felt as if she was raining inside, and the mud which flew out from under the wheels of her car was as churned as her innermost feelings.

She ran up the three steps to the door of the little annexe which she'd had built on, and fitted the key into the lock, and after she had telephoned Patsy she put through a call to the Centre.

'Any urgent calls? I'm just back from Anita Boughton's—she's okay.'

'Yes, so Dr Radcliffe said. Of course, you wouldn't know——'

'I didn't, but I do now,' Fiona cut in crisply. 'Hell of a way to start back, and what weather!' she added more congenially. 'I'm going to call in to see Anita's mother on my way in, by which time you'll have collected a few messages I expect.'

'There are one or two, but nothing that can't wait.

Take your time,' said Doreen, the head receptionist.

Fiona replaced the receiver and rubbed her head as she surveyed her lounge floor. She could have done with the day off to sort out the contents of her case, do her laundry, and have time to reflect on this unbidden situation, but it might be better if she put all her energy into the day's work. She knew that if she had the opportunity she would curl up in an easy chair and try to sort out her muddled thoughts.

With some impatience at having to leave the lounge so disorganised she went to her small, modern bathroom and had a shower in the unit which was tucked away in the corner behind the door, then she dressed in a green and maroon coloured plaid wool skirt, and teamed it up with a dark green jumper. Her cords weren't all that wet, but suddenly it was important to look as presentable as she could. Her hair could have done with a quick wash, but it was likely to get a soaking today so the shampoo would be more beneficial when she finished work. While she collected the necessary requirements for her brief-case she made a cup of black coffee, and by the time she was ready, complete with smart tan shoes, stylish yet comfortable, the coffee was cool enough to drink, and she set off again, this time towards Kenelm, stopping off at a modern bungalow where Mrs Craven, Anita's mother, lived.

'No serious damage, but of course she's in a fair amount of pain,' Fiona explained. 'If she needs more pain-killers let me know and I'll get a prescription for her. She was rather frightened, especially as she was carrying Lucy, but the doctor checked her over and she seems all right.'

'Why ever didn't she ring me straight away?' Mrs Craven said. 'No need to bother you busy people.'

'I suspect she panicked. Probably thought she'd broken something.'

'Thank goodness she hasn't. Don't you worry, Fiona, I'll see to Anita now. It'll give our Catherine something to do when she comes back from the Job Centre. Thanks, anyway.'

Fiona pulled the hood of her anorak up over her head and ran back to her car.

She parked in her allotted space at the health centre and had to hold her head down against the violent wind and rain as she picked her way between puddles to the entrance. As she pushed the swing door with her shoulder someone else pulled it open from inside and she fell against a large masculine frame.

Stephen steadied her, and then with some impatience said: 'I told you we'd bump into one another—I didn't mean literally,' and he went past her out into the wild weather.

CHAPTER TWO

FIONA, with her anorak hood shielding her face from view, watched Stephen pull his raincoat round his body and hurry the few yards to his Rover. Then she shook her head free and walked into the reception and waiting area where the three receptionists, Doreen, Betty and Sylvia, called patients' names, answered the telephones and dealt with a variety of enquiries from repeat prescriptions to X-ray and test results, as well as requests for house calls. Fiona passed by unnoticed, up the stairs to a large airy office which bore a nameplate: HEALTH VISITORS. She had just removed her anorak and was hanging it on the back of the door when it opened and James Coudray entered.

'Darling!' His enthusiasm took her breath away, as he hugged and kissed her. 'No more ten-day courses for you, I can't live without you,' he whispered.

Fiona broke away to slam the door. 'How did you know I was in?'

'I asked Doreen to buzz me.'

'But I don't believe anyone noticed me,' she protested. 'It's Monday morning—and bedlam.'

'Not for me,' James said, squeezing her waist. 'It's heaven, you're back. When Doreen buzzed me she said you'd just collided with Dr Locke's replacement.'

'Oh, yes, *that*! I suppose it was inevitable that such a collision wouldn't go unnoticed. Actually I met him at Anita Boughton's.'

'So I believe. Stephen gave me all the information.'

20

'Actually——' she began.

'Stephen and I are old acquaintances,' James hurried on. Wasn't that exactly what she had been about to say! 'When he was a houseman, I got a post as senior registrar at Bristol. He emigrated to Australia soon afterwards though, so I didn't know him all that well. Rumour had it that his fiancée jilted him, but he must have married eventually as he's recently been widowed. Three young children too, such a tragedy.'

Fiona escaped from James' hold and went to her desk where she'd placed her shoulder bag. She took out a comb and vigorously dragged it through her tight waves. Wet weather made it quite unmanageable so it was the best she could do and it helped to soften the blow that James knew something of Stephen's past, which left her speechless. She ought to have come right out with the truth there and then, that she was the fiancée who had jilted him, but it sounded so cold, calculating and cruel, and only she knew the whole truth. If she intended to accept James' proposal of marriage, which he had taken for granted, she would have to tell him the full story. The right time will present itself, she reassured herself, trying to appease her guilt, and maybe Stephen would think twice about staying now that he had come face to face with her, but James soon corrected that supposition.

'Sorry you had the nasty shock of hearing about Dr Locke from a total stranger. I know you had a special affinity with him—well, he was the father of us all—but maybe it's all working out rather well. Stephen Radcliffe is familiar with this area. His parents live over at Gorton, but he's not decided where to settle yet so we must all do some persuading. His parents' house is that great mansion of a place on the south road out of Gorton. I'm sure you must know it, darling. His father has been a consultant at Gorton County Hospital for years.'

'Yes, I know it, but maybe he's got other ideas. Perhaps he doesn't want to be a GP. I imagine he had some plum job in Australia.'

'Top consultant in orthopaedics.' James was studying her closely as she opened her briefcase. 'He has a nanny for the children but he feels as a family they'll benefit from his parents' influence. The house has a separate wing on one side which he intends living in when all his possessions arrive from Australia.'

'Losing his wife must have been a shattering experience. It'll take time to readjust, then perhaps he'll change his mind,' she said hopefully.

'Sounds as if you aren't keen on him. Not impressed?' James asked with a puzzled frown.

Fiona shrugged indifferently. 'You surely can't have finished your list?' she said, changing the subject.

'No—but I was anxious to see you. Stephen's wife died some time ago, Fiona. He's had time to adjust. His contract ran out; he could have renewed it but he suddenly felt he needed to return to grass roots, and have a change from orthopaedics. I think he probably has some idea of where he's going, and for our centre it couldn't have been better timed.'

'I must hurry, I've got my clinic this afternoon, though if this weather continues I shouldn't think many will turn out. How's Cassie?'

'I thought you'd never ask.' James smiled affectionately. 'She's well and happy. I won't spoil it by saying she didn't miss you, but she'll be one very contented lady when we name the day and get married.'

'Don't rush me, James, please.'

'Absence should make the heart grow fonder. I'd hoped you'd have rushed straight into my arms the moment you returned.' He sounded disappointed and Fiona felt herself flushing a little.

'It was dreadfully late, James,' she excused.

'You didn't even phone, or write,' he scolded.

'I didn't promise I would.' She sounded tetchy, but she couldn't help herself.

He was scrutinising her again, embarrassing her. 'Welcome home, anyway, darling. I'll bring Cassie round this evening.'

'Don't bother. I can go and pick her up when I finish my clinic.'

James sauntered to the door, turned, and with a hesitant smile said, 'She'll be locked in the house while I'm doing my evening surgery so I'll see you at about eight.'

Fiona sat down heavily on her chair as the door closed softly. She sat with her head in her hands for a few moments. This wasn't the way she had meant to return. She had been looking forward to seeing James again, and she couldn't think why she hadn't said that she'd telephoned three times but could get no reply. She was half afraid of whatever it was that made her reluctant to tell him about the past, and convinced that her answer to his proposal must be no. It was this new fear that made her feel like screaming. No, she didn't want to see James tonight. Yes, it was going to be one hell of a day!

Fiona went downstairs a few minutes later and collected her messages book. While she was at Reception she glanced at the doctors' pad but there was nothing there which directly affected her.

'I'll be in for half an hour, Doreen, then I'll be out visiting until one o'clock, back in time to get ready for my mother and baby clinic,' she said.

'There's a big bag full of children's clothing in Lizzie's room,' Doreen said. 'The locum brought them in, said his mother decided his children all needed different clothing for this climate. He's recently returned from Australia so I expect they need a lot of warmer things.'

'Oh, thanks, anything's welcome.' Fiona went back up the open beechwood stairs. She'd never escape Stephen now, as long as he was in the district. A new doctor was always a good topic for conversation and Stephen Radcliffe was handsome enough to warrant comment. She could hardly believe that the vision she had kept alive in her memory could be so accurate. His hair might be a shade lighter but was still wavy, perhaps not quite as unruly as it had once been, and there were traces of grey appearing at his temples. The climate in Australia would have toned down the intense blackness, she supposed, and his recent tragedy would have caused some grey hairs to appear. Though not so recent, according to James. He had been a widower for some while, whatever that might mean. Her imagination was quick to present a picture of a church and cemetery with Stephen standing at an open graveside, his broad shoulders hunched in grief. No matter what he thought of her she could feel every painful emotion for him, and was genuinely sympathetic at his personal tragedy even though she didn't know the circumstances of his wife's death.

While she was compiling a list of visits Patsy breezed into the office. 'Anita's mum's arrived and has taken over,' she announced. 'A lot of fuss about nothing if you ask me.'

'She was concerned about Lucy,' Fiona replied with mild rebuke, 'and Anita does have a very swollen ankle. Better to have yelled for help than try to cope, only to discover either the baby or herself did have some injury.'

'Oh, you, the virtuous one,' Patsy sang light-heartedly, 'and on a Monday morning. Don't you *ever* blow your top?'

'Frequently—usually to poor old Cass. She can't answer back.' Fiona's expression relaxed into a gentle smile. 'Anything to report from the last ten days?' she asked.

'Mm—mother and baby clinics were okay, and there were about four new cases, two of them were second and third babies, all fine, and being attended to by Meg, our highly esteemed midwife, the others——'

'Patsy?' Fiona asked, her brow creased in apprehensive curiosity. 'What have you been up to? Not trying to tell Meggie her job, I hope?'

'As if I would.'

'Patsy dear—I know you're a qualified nurse, but diplomacy doesn't seem to be your strong point. Meggie is a very experienced midwife and it's not your prerogative to question anything she advises.'

'So are you a qualified midwife,' Patsy retorted.

'But not as experienced as Meggie. I hope I haven't got to follow up all your visits to try to make the peace like I did last time?'

'No, of course not.' Patsy suddenly became thoughtful and quiet.

'I'll have to know, and I'm sure Meggie will love telling me,' Fiona prompted.

'It's Mrs Pines—her baby is going through the yelling stages. It's her own fault, she won't leave it alone. She's terrified of cot-death so she wakes it up to make sure it's all right.'

'And where does Meggie come into this?'

'Sue Pines telephoned her. She doesn't like me, so Meggie tried to pacify her and then had a go at me and said I'm no good as a health visitor because

I'm not sympathetic enough.'

'Mrs Pines' attitude and worry is normal behaviour in a new mother, as you should know by now, Patsy.'

'But she's obsessive, and that's unnatural,' Patsy pouted.

'Every mother accepts her new responsibilities in a different way. Some women have babies, even the first, get up, and take to motherhood with no qualms or problems. Every case is individual. Quite a lot of women are terrified of the new life that *she* is responsible for.'

'I knew you'd take Meggie's side,' Patsy complained.

'It isn't a question of sides, Patsy,' Fiona insisted. 'Our job is to try to allay fears and insecurity. Have you forgotten *everything* you were taught?'

'I did try to help Sue, but she's morose one minute, aggressive the next.'

'Which means she needs help. I'd better go there first.' Fiona sighed. 'Means another trip back to Avon Vale estate.' She wrote the name on her pad.

'The locum's dishy. *I* was the first one to meet him,' Patsy crowed.

'I'm sure he was impressed.'

'It's no wonder you're not married, Fiona—you're *so*—so—indifferent.' When Fiona failed to respond to the bait Patsy hurried on, 'I was just coming in one lunch time before clinic and he was hovering, looking for Dr Coudray. I hope he stays for good, he's a widower with three children.'

'Poor man,' Fiona mumbled, 'little does he know how he's being torn to shreds.'

'You can scoff,' Patsy retorted, 'and I suppose you think he won't notice me because I'm too young, but lots of men marry a much younger woman the second time.'

'Oh? You're so knowledgeable, Patsy—but I think

it's time to get to work. Let's see what you've organised for today.'

Together they went through the age register and Patsy was given a list of elderly to visit, while Fiona set off to visit Sue Pines and two new mothers whose details had just reached the Centre. As she drove away she considered Patsy's future. Normally Fiona coped with the younger girl's ebullience without irritation, but today was anything but a normal day, and it was Monday. At least Patsy was safe enough visiting the elderly. She was good with them and they seemed to appreciate her exuberant sense of fun. It was seldom that any of the over seventy-fives complained about her, yet Fiona was frequently having to make excuses to the young mothers, some of whom were about the same age as Patsy. She was a sophisticated twenty-two-year-old, almost ten years to the day Fiona's junior. It seemed to question the validity of horoscopes as their birthdays were within three days of each other in October, though Patsy was a cusp, so maybe that accounted for their different temperaments, and yet they worked compatibly most of the time.

A health visitor's work consisted largely of listening, which was just as well, Fiona decided, when she found herself sitting in Sue Pines' dining-room being treated to a fair old barrel of abuse.

'That girl's just too young to be a health visitor,' she blurted angrily. 'How can she know how a mother feels, and what can she possibly know about bringing up a baby?' She paused for breath, and the very fact that Fiona didn't rush to Patsy's defence made her continue on a second wind. 'Blasted welfare workers, you're all the same. You all think you know it all, that you're right, that you've got all the answers, and look at you—no kids of your own so what the hell would you know about it?'

For the first time Fiona was obliged to lower her gaze. That was the kind of hurtful remark she found difficult to take. She doubted that she'd have been any more of a perfect mother than anyone else, but she'd have given anything—yes, even the proverbial right arm—for the chance to find out. If she'd lost a limb in that car crash at least she would have been able to give Stephen the children they'd planned for—now, some other woman had given him those, and Fiona felt sick inside at her inadequacy. Over the years she had bravely come to terms with her lot, but Stephen was back, here in Kenelm, which could only mean embarrassment for both of them, and her wound ripped open.

'Sue, I'm sorry you've been having problems and that Patsy couldn't help,' she sympathised patiently.

'Help! How can anyone help? The baby never cries when any of you lot are here.'

'Are you managing to get some sleep yourself? Perhaps you're run down. Why don't you have a check-up with one of the doctors?'

'Because it's such a hassle to get the baby ready, and myself, for an appointment. I can't cope with organisation any more. I want Daniel to sleep but when he does I have to keep checking, and if I can't see him breathing I pick him up quickly.' She dragged her hands down her face in desperation and Fiona knew it wouldn't take much to bring a flood of tears.

'Can I see him, Sue?'

'If you must. Patsy says I've made him a light sleeper because I fuss so much.'

'Let's go and have a look. I'll be extra quiet.' She slipped off her shoes and wet anorak then followed Sue up the stairs, noticing how slim the young mother was.

Fiona knew from previous visits that Daniel was a bonny baby with black, expressive eyes alert to everything going on in the big wide world, and now she looked down on him, passive enough in sleep, with admiration.

Fiona leaned over the cot side and smiled. 'He's grown since I saw him last at the clinic,' she whispered. There was no response and when she turned Sue had disappeared. Fiona could hear muffled sobs coming from the largest of three bedrooms.

'He's fine, Sue,' she reassured gently, 'and he's sleeping peacefully now. Why don't you get yourself back to bed for an hour. You're worn out—with worry mostly.'

'I shall go into a deep sleep. I shan't hear Daniel wake.'

'I'm sure you will. He must have a very healthy cry by now.'

'But supposing he suffocates, or can't breathe while I'm asleep?'

Fiona sat down on the bed beside her. 'It's sleep you need, Sue. If Daniel cries it'll eventually wake you, and he's not going to suffocate. You've covered him sensibly without overdoing it, your house is comfortably warm and he's lying on his tummy; he's safe enough,' she said.

'He might roll over on to his back.'

'More than likely, but that doesn't matter. Sue, you're worrying unnecessarily about him. It's true there are inexplicable cot deaths, the reason for which hasn't as yet been identified, but we have to accept such things. It's no use losing sleep waiting for something to happen which, please God, never will. I think you should have a check-up with one of the doctors. A tonic might help you to cope more easily. Try to get to my clinic every week where you'll meet other mothers like yourself. Come for a cup of tea and a chat.'

'They're all so young—like Patsy in their early twenties or younger. Do you realise I shall be thirty this year?' She sounded hysterical.

'Age makes little difference except perhaps that you take things more seriously, but you must keep everything in its right perspective, Sue. I'm thirty-two and I'd love to have a baby like Daniel. He's growing stronger every day, progressing well even if it isn't apparent to you. Soon there'll be teeth to worry him, then you can expect to walk the floor a time or two. I'm sure there's nothing wrong with either him or you. Let's go and have a cup of tea.'

Fiona stayed longer than she should have, but Sue did need her and she brightened up and was grateful for the support. Fiona then had to move on at a reasonable speed and was pleased to find that the two new mothers of first babies had returned home after ten days in hospital with no problems in evidence. In both cases the husbands were on holiday from work for a week to get accustomed to their new status of fatherhood, and both seemed domestically capable, which helped.

Back at the Centre Patsy was already putting out the weighing scales, chairs and screens in readiness for the afternoon session.

'There's bags of clothes, children's and adults', over there in the corner. Doreen said Dr Radcliffe brought them in.'

'We can always find needy families for things like that. Perhaps if we have a quiet few minutes you can start sorting it.'

Fiona couldn't bring herself to even look at it yet, though she knew it was up to her to decide where it was allocated. Now she was being foolish, she told herself crossly. As if a few items of clothing belonging to

Stephen's children could have any effect on her! She was seeing babies and children continuously and it had helped in the past to counteract the fact that she could never have any of her own, but she hadn't reckoned with having to meet Stephen's family. She almost prayed that he wouldn't remain long in Gorton, she didn't think she could stand it.

'I'll just go along for a cup of tea and a sandwich in the canteen,' she said to Patsy, but the moment she opened the door she wished she hadn't. Stephen was there sitting at a table with Dr Laura O'Neal.

Fiona tried not to notice them as she went to the counter and asked Katie for a cup of tea and a ham sandwich, but as soon as she turned to look for a vacant table Laura called her over.

'Come and meet Dr Radcliffe, Fiona.'

'We've already met,' she answered quickly.

'Well come and sit with us anyway. You're later than usual, for a Monday.'

Stephen half stood, and pulled out the chair on one of the vacant sides of the small square table. 'Didn't get off to a very good start did you, Fiona?' Was his voice especially mellow for her benefit or was she imagining things? 'We met at my first emergency house call this morning,' he explained to Laura.

'Anything serious?' Laura asked.

'No. Anita Boughton fell down the last three or four stairs with Lucy in her arms. She's hurt her ankle, otherwise they both appear to be all right.'

'Is it usual for doctors to make house calls at the same time as health visitors?' Stephen asked.

'No,' Fiona replied softly but firmly. 'She panicked and rang here. Someone evidently decided a doctor was needed, and when they told her I was back she rang me as well. She was in shock and that's what I'm here for.'

'It was rather a waste of a call. You got there before me and you could have decided whether a doctor need see her or not.'

'That is how it usually works,' Fiona said calmly.

'But not today?'

Laura laughed. 'The system isn't without faults,' she said, sensing that the new doctor was averse to health visitors.

Lots of doctors were. Fiona was never sure whether they regarded the service as an unnecessary expense or whether they felt it put their jobs at risk, but over the years at Kenelm Health Centre a good liaison had been established between herself and the team of five doctors. Of course, she thought silently, with dear Dr Locke at the helm there could only be harmony. The younger doctors came in determined to change everything with their new-fangled up-to-date ideas, but Dr Locke and his wealth of experience had been a competent match for any of them.

Laura stood up. 'Stephen's going to sit in on our clinic session today, Fiona. It'll be a good opportunity for him to meet some of the young mums he'll have on his list.'

Stephen nodded his excuses as he followed Laura, and Fiona was thankful to be left alone. So, already Dr Locke's list had become Stephen's. That didn't sound much like a temporary arrangement, it had a permanent ring to it and her mind galloped ahead with visions of her packing up and heading for the North of England. But, wasn't she going to marry James?

The afternoon passed quickly. It was rewarding to see the young mothers' expressions as they watched Patsy or Fiona weigh their babies, though Fiona's main job was to sit in a warm corner of the room where she chatted to the young women, and listened attentively to their problems. She kept thinking of Sue Pines and her accusations, knowing that it must seem ironical to many mothers that their advising health visitors had no personal experience of babies to draw on. Fiona tried never to preach, never to be too adamant about her advice, but rather taking the line, 'well, shall we try so and so?' and in most cases it worked.

Today she tried not to think of Stephen working with Laura in the adjoining room checking babies at six weeks old, six months or a year. She didn't need to come into contact with them as they could enter and leave by a door from the consulting and examination rooms. She wondered what Stephen thought of the health centre. It was a very well designed building with the Elizabeth Nursery Suite especially endowed by Dr Locke's late mother, and affectionately called 'Lizzie's' rooms, conveniently on the ground floor with separate entrances and a large spacious hall to accommodate prams and pushchairs.

Katie, who managed the staff canteen, had a special second serving hatch into a small room in the Elizabeth Nursery Suite, and being the mother of five children, ages ranging from seven to fifteen, she loved every minute of making tea and sometimes serving homemade cakes on clinic afternoons.

There couldn't be anywhere in the world nicer to work, Fiona had always felt, where the community spirit was such that the inhabitants of Kenelm were of one mind to work for the benefit of their health centre.

At her ten-day course she had proclaimed with no inhibitions the values of village and rural districts for ideal working conditions, but now her personal happiness had taken a real blow. How was it going to affect her future?

CHAPTER THREE

THE wind had dropped, and the rain decreased to a light misty drizzle so as the afternoon progressed more mothers with babies and toddlers arrived, and the session passed quickly, even over-running by nearly an hour.

Patsy stacked up the chairs, Katie closed up the serving hatch on the nursery suite side, and Fiona put away notes and files in her briefcase.

'We shan't have time to sort out those clothes today, Patsy,' she said. 'Put them in the top of the cupboard and hopefully we'll have a slack day to sort and allocate it all. There'll be spring jumble sales at the local village halls soon so we shall get another load for sure.'

'I hope you'll be able to find a use for the outgrown clothing.' Fiona looked up to see Stephen standing in the doorway. 'I believe I have to give you these?'

Fiona took the pile of cards from him. 'Thanks,' she said, trying to avoid looking directly into his eyes. Too many memories were reflected there. 'Yes, I'm sure they'll be most welcome. We have a gypsy encampment up on the barrow. They don't like us much, but do find our good, used clothing useful.' She managed a nervous laugh.

Stephen slowly advanced to her table. 'Finished for the day?'

'A bit of paperwork to do upstairs before I leave.'

Fiona was aware of Patsy rooted to the spot watching with interest. She felt herself trembling a little and knew that she sounded strange, then Laura O'Neal came in buttoning her raincoat.

'That's that done,' she said, 'no surgery for either of us this evening so we'll see you tomorrow.'

Stephen had no option but to accompany her away from the nursery suite.

'He isn't going to be a widower for long,' Patsy mumbled. 'Trust Laura to make a play for him.'

'Laura has a husband,' Fiona reminded her.

'So she says, but no one's ever seen him. I reckon they're separated.'

'He works abroad, Patsy.'

'Trust you to believe that story. You're so naive, Fiona. Still, won't be long before you're Mrs Coudray, so rumour has it.'

'Don't waste your time romancing about other people,' Fiona warned, 'or you'll miss the boat yourself.'

'Oh, no one ever looks twice at me. I'm either too thin or too fat—depending how my eating habits are at the time, and when I meet someone I really fancy I go and say the most stupid things.'

'You're probably trying too hard, and you still need to mature a bit, but Mr Right will come along eventually.'

'Like he hasn't for you,' Patsy jibed. 'Though I must say our new Doc had a certain interested glint in his eye.'

'Pure imagination,' Fiona answered back, and left to go up to her office.

She called at Reception on her way for any new calls, and just as she approached the stairs she heard James' voice. Fiona turned to greet him.

'You're in early,' she said.

'Sure—got a date tonight,' and he winked saucily as he went to his consulting room.

The early evening patients were beginning to arrive

and Fiona was prevented from pursuing the conversation, but she did wish she could have put James off. She supposed everyone knew of their relationship and up until now it hadn't mattered, but she suddenly found she wanted to deny the rumours of an imminent wedding. They tried to keep their private lives shielded from onlookers and the public gaze, but being colleagues didn't make it easy and the rest of the team seemed to have cottoned on to the situation rapidly in spite of being told that after Dr Locke, James and Fiona were the two old hands, in at the very beginning of Kenelm's health centre. Laura O'Neal was a comparative newcomer, Fiona's rival for James some thought, but Fiona preferred to believe that she was already happily married. Brian Sandford had been appointed nearly four years ago, and Perry Linnell, a bachelor, two years later. In spite of being the junior partner he was the popular one and assured of full surgeries. Everyone teased him about being the attainable bachelor, and although he was fond of women, and was suave and good-looking, he was a genuinely nice man devoted to his profession. When he had first arrived at the Centre he had shown more than a passing interest in Fiona, but he quickly backed off when he saw how her relationship with James was developing. She had tried hard to keep it on a friendship basis but dear Dr Locke had done everything he could to encourage it without openly admitting to his little schemes. Intimate dinner parties seemingly arranged just for Fiona and James, and at some large town seminars the wily old doctor detailed Fiona to accompany James, and so rather than falling head over heels in love with each other they had drifted into a happy, genuinely close relationship.

After an hour in the office listening to Patsy's report of

her morning visits to some of the elderly, and dealing with the various problems that reached the health visitors' desk via the doctors or receptionists, district nurse or social worker, Fiona was glad when she could put her coat on and lock up the office. The evenings were gradually beginning to get lighter, but today being so damp and miserable made it seem as if winter had returned. Even the daffodils and tulips were hanging their heads in limp surrender.

Nothing had enchanted her first day home and she had to admit to feeling weary. She drove her car into the open-ended garage and looked at her bedraggled flower border which edged the path to the back door. Inside she took off her anorak and hung it up on the back of the door before going through to her pine-wood kitchen. If she had been eating alone she'd have settled for a pizza as she'd enjoyed a little over-indulgence during the past week not having to cook for herself, but there was James to consider now. The freezer and microwave oven had been purchased for convenience, and after a few moments pondering over the contents of the freezer she selected steaks—no—she might need those for a special occasion; chops, liver and bacon with oven-ready chips and peas would do for James.

As she prepared it all she very nearly changed her mind. James being her guest and intended future husband, she should have had no hesitation in choosing the steaks, especially as they were his favourite, she rebuked herself. But suddenly her visions had changed and she pictured herself with Stephen sitting down to a candle-lit dinner for two. She sighed in contempt of her feelings. It was obvious that Stephen didn't have a very good opinion of her so it was hardly likely that he would ever deign to visit her home. She doubted that he would

approve of her mobile home-cum-bungalow. She remembered how single-minded he had been in their
plans—at least four children once he had become an
established consultant, with a large rural house which
must stand in acres of woodland. Fiona glanced out of
her lounge window which overlooked her fair-sized
lawn, and beyond the high chain-link fencing she could
wallow in the most generous view of the forest—tall
evergreen trees with pine-needled avenues where
people taking riding lessons from the nearby stables
cantered and trotted in isolated tranquillity.

She sat with a cup of tea to watch the news on
television, glad of the warmth of her home. Being away
had meant it seemed cold and damp on her return so she
had left the central heating on at a low setting throughout the day and now, having drawn the velvet curtains it
felt snug. She tackled the job of unpacking her suitcase
and bags, and when the place looked presentable again
she opened the extension on her oak drop-leaf table and
covered it with a dainty embroidered cloth. James had
shown his delight in having her back so she placed her
two silver flower candle-holders on each end of the table
and put the pale green candles in the fridge so that they
would burn more slowly. With her stone-coloured
pottery ware, designed with a harvest scene of corn and
bright red poppies, the table looked attractive. She set
out two wine goblets as she was certain that wine would
be James' contribution, a lovely red claret which would
have been ideally suitable to complement the steaks.

This was a new experience to feel guilty about her
relationship with James. She had vowed never to become involved with another man. Stephen had been her
life, her all, and she had sacrificed her personal happiness for his, believing she knew how devastated he

would feel at her not being able to bear his children. She was genuinely sorry about his wife, but at least she had given him what he wanted. He had intimated that he'd suffered two great tragedies in his life but he did have a family and had been able to enjoy ten years of happy family life. She was glad about that for nothing could erase memories, just as nothing and no one could ever dim the memories of their short but blissful engagement. It was only the passing of time and Fiona's maturity which had inclined her towards an understanding with James. He hadn't asked questions but accepted her explanation that following a car accident she found she was unable to have children. Only Dr Locke knew the full facts, but now after all this time it wouldn't matter as no one was likely to read up her history. James would be the senior partner so Dr Locke's list would become his, though because of their relationship and certainly if they married she would have to be treated by one of the others. Fiona sighed. She must pray that Stephen would move on, that he would find the situation as intolerable as she did.

The meal was ready, the candle flames casting a romantic glow and intimate shadows over the room, when she heard James' car. She went out to the annexe, a large old bath towel in her hands ready to catch Cassie who bounded in ahead of James.

Cassie didn't approve of being dried when her prime aim was to greet her mistress with boisterous affection and it was some minutes before she calmed down.

'I didn't feed her, darling,' James said as he kissed Fiona's flushed cheek. 'In spite of the weather she's had several good runs today and when we came to the site entrance I let her out and she ran home.'

'Thanks for having her, James. I'd hate the thought of

her going into kennels. I know she'd be well looked after but she's young, she needs a lot of love.'

'Like her owner,' James said in a seductive tone which today irritated her.

Fiona got to her feet and went into the kitchen.

'I'll give Cass hers first then she'll be quiet while we're eating.'

If James noticed the lack of response to his comment he didn't pursue the matter but took off his jacket and went through to the lounge.

'Fiona—this is lovely. I only expected a snack meal.'

'I thought you'd be hungry, being that I haven't been here to feed you,' she replied with a quick smile of guilt-ridden reparation.

'I've been well looked after. Laura invited me for a meal.' At Fiona's direct glance he hurried on with hands held high. 'I refused, for the sake of protocol.'

'You didn't need to refuse a meal on my account.'

'I hope that means that you have implicit faith in me, darling. Laura likes male company and if I'd accepted I'd have felt duty bound to take her out for a meal at a later date—then tongues might have started wagging.'

'I wouldn't have minded,' Fiona said from the kitchen where she was dishing up.

A shadow fell across the pine-wood table where two hot plates were laden with appetising meat and vegetables.

James took the pan of peas from her hand, turned her round and held her shoulders firmly. 'I hope you would have. I want you to trust me, but I want you to care.'

'In a place like this tongues will always wag—in any case, Laura has a husband.'

James ended the conversation by drawing her against his chest, teasing her with lightly spilled kisses over her forehead, eyes, ears and cheeks until he demanded some responses from her lips.

She broke away as soon as it was prudent to do so and hurried the plates to the dining-table.

'Laura doesn't seem to be very forthcoming about this husband of hers, and I notice she's befriending Stephen Radcliffe. He seems to have knitted in with everyone and everything extremely quickly,' James said.

'He is a local man,' Fiona said, 'so I understand.'

Now why had she added that? Why did she feel so guilty at knowing Stephen, and why couldn't she own up now to this slice of the past which had come back to taunt her? She felt her cheeks glow uncomfortably red and she hurried back to the kitchen without an excuse while James uncorked the claret, and when she returned he handed her a glass.

'Try it, Madame,' he joked, 'and if it's not to your liking we'll get the wine waiter to change it.'

'We won't put the wine waiter to so much trouble as it's such a rotten night.' She sipped daintily. 'It's lovely, James. I'm sorry it's such a poor meal.'

'A mixed grill? Don't you know I'm only marrying you for your cooking?'

As gallant as ever he took her drink and placed it on the coaster, then held her chair and pushed it in as she sat down.

'Romantic dinner by candlelight,' he mused. 'I must remember not to talk shop.'

There were a few minutes of sombre silence broken only by the chink of cutlery, then Fiona asked; 'How is Dr Locke?'

'Stable, but paralysed quite extensively. His speech is badly impaired at present, but in time his condition may improve.' His tone was without conviction.

'I must go to see him and Mrs Locke. How's she coping?'

'Very well—like most doctors' wives they learn over the years to cope with all manner of crises.'

'That's a mere fact of life for most people regardless of job or profession. She's quite frail really though, isn't she?'

'But strong-willed and tough in spirit.'

'He's still in hospital I take it?'

'Yes, but he'll soon be moved to a private nursing home where they can concentrate on the remedial nursing. I expect it's better it should happen this way than that he just got old and doddery.'

'I can't imagine Dr Locke ever becoming old and doddery,' Fiona said with affection in her voice.

'We've been lucky, darling. He's kept alert, and has been our store of experience, but he had to retire eventually.'

'I somehow can't imagine the district without him. You become the senior partner automatically, I suppose?'

'Mm—more or less, after a few formalities. We had a meeting last week and my name was put forward, no one appeared to object, and then Stephen's name came up as locum, but it would be splendid if we can get him permanently.'

'Perhaps he won't want to be permanent as he and his father are well-known in the area.'

'By what he said, his mother expects him to stay. After all, he's been abroad for nearly ten years.'

Yes, of course Mrs Radcliffe would be overjoyed to have him back, and now she could indulge her grand-children, even though she already had four or five from her other son, Simon, and younger daughter, Penny. A much older daughter, Margaret, still unmarried, was also a doctor for a missionary society and was seldom at home. Neither Simon nor Penny and their respective families lived in the vicinity so, Fiona reasoned, Stephen's parents would be particularly pleased to have him resident in the big family house. At least that was a reasonable distance from Kenelm, and Fiona hoped their paths might only cross at the Centre.

'Have you returned to lots of problems, Fiona?' James's deep voice splintered her thoughts into tiny fragments of the past and present. 'We all kept our eye on Patsy. How do you feel she's making out?'

Health visitors had a central governing body of their own and were not directly responsible to the doctors at the health centre, but liaison was vitally important and unlike some doctors James was amenable to the health visitors and the work they did, so he took an interest in Patsy. She was well qualified but young and in many respects had not yet learned the art of listening to patients' problems, when and when not to voice her own opinion.

'Nothing too awful, but Sue Pines called in Meggie because she didn't feel Patsy was much help.'

'Why does she need help?'

'She's terrified that baby Daniel will suffocate. It's becoming an obsession—in that I do agree with Patsy, though I didn't say so, but it's more than that, James. Sue seems too tired to cope, she needs a tonic or a course of iron.'

'I see,' James said drily, 'doing my job for me, are you?'

'No—you know I'm not—it's only a suggestion. Sue really had a go at me about health and welfare visitors in general, but Patsy in particular.'

'You know I'm a great fan of health visitors and I'm confident that in our Centre we've created the ideal set-up, so I don't want to see all your good work damaged by Patsy's lack of experience.'

'If she doesn't do the job she can't gain the experience. Some people think I'm not much help because I just sit and listen, but when it comes down to the nitty gritty that's probably all I can do for some of the patients, and it's all *they* want—someone to sound off to.'

'I know you had reservations at the start because you felt you might be too well-known here, but it hasn't proved to be a stumbling block, has it?'

'No, but then I'd been away several years doing my general nursing and midwifery training before the special HV course. Patsy is really doing her stuff with the elderly in the area, I'm not that well-known to the majority of young mothers.'

'I suppose you must know of the Radcliffe family?'

Fiona almost fell over Cassie as she got up from the table in confusion.

'I must just see to the coffee perking—I can hear it boiling.'

Fortunately James seemed to be enjoying his meal too much to notice that his question went unanswered, and when Fiona returned to sit down opposite him he was eager to recount the amusing antics of Cassie, and to hear details of Fiona's course. She silently prayed that he wouldn't mention the Radcliffes, and Stephen in particular. The rest of the evening passed pleasantly and it was barely eleven when James finished his nightcap and prepared to leave.

'By the way, Fiona, I heard a rather disturbing piece of council gossip today. Kenelm Primary School is earmarked for the chop.'

'Oh, *no*! Surely not. They can't *do* that! Can they, James?'

He raised his eyebrows sympathetically. 'I'm afraid they can if there aren't enough children to warrant keeping it going.'

'But there are loads of new babies.'

'Yes, darling, *babies*, but before they get to school age the families move on to a larger house—new job—that's the price we have to pay for unemployment. Years ago folk were content to stay in one area, but I'm afraid things have changed.'

'We're going to fight it—aren't we?'

James inclined his head and smiled apologetically. 'It is a *very* old school, Fiona. It needs modernising.'

'It's a lovely school, warm and cosy. It *can't* close,' she added hotly.

James enclosed her in a warm embrace. 'I love your sentiments, darling, but in this day and age we have to be realistic.' She allowed him to indulge in a few tender kisses, though they, and she, lacked any real passion, and a few moments later she was left alone, angry at the news he had just passed on, and irritated that he appeared to be unmoved by the implications.

By Wednesday afternoon when the practice meeting was held Fiona had heard the rumour from a few more reliable sources. Several young mothers had also heard and already a petition was set up, Fiona's name at the head of the list, and she went to the meeting armed with a clip-board. She hid it under her notebook and files on the table while Stephen was officially welcomed into the practice.

'I'm counting on all of you to help Stephen as much as possible in the hope we can persuade him to join us on a permanent basis,' James said.

'Thank you, James,' Stephen answered, 'you've all made me feel very much at home already—well, this is home, or at least a return to grass roots, but that's the reason why I feel I cannot make a decision about permanency yet awhile. I must have a few weeks to settle down. It's not necessarily a good thing to work, especially this kind of work, where you grew up and have past connections.'

Fiona felt the blood drain from her cheeks. He meant her, of course, and she knew that his dark eyes, hooded by smooth black eyebrows, were continuously glancing in her direction.

'Fiona has never found it a problem, have you?' James asked.

Fiona was doodling in nervous panic on her pad, but she managed to raise her gaze to meet James'.

'Not that I recall,' she said, 'but then I've been back six years now.'

'It depends on the circumstances,' Stephen said coldly, and when Fiona dared to glance across the table at him their eyes focused on each other in the kind of intimate look from which it was impossible to retract.

There were those who would remember about us, he seemed to be reminding her. Old rumours would be revived, too many memories would be reborn to kindle anew suspicion as to what had occurred between them. By going away to take her midwifery course when she had sufficiently recovered from her injuries, Fiona had managed to avoid sympathy from the local inhabitants, and when she had returned six years ago she imagined that the past had been buried. But now with the reappearance of Stephen there was a risk of the ashes being raked over.

CHAPTER FOUR

'I'M sure the advantages must outweigh the disadvantages,' James said, with a laugh.

Surely he and everyone else round that table must have recognised some hidden liaison between her and Stephen. Fiona wished she had some plausible excuse for hurrying away, but she was duty bound to remain.

'It's not a valid reason for not staying, Stephen,' Laura O'Neal put in sweetly.

'Are we certain that Dr Locke won't be returning?' Perry asked.

He would never know how grateful Fiona was for his intervention, for it led to the latest medical bulletin on the much loved senior partner's condition, and then Meggie, the district nurse and midwife, did her best to hurry the agenda along to patients' needs.

'Old Mrs Hartnell could do with a visit from you, Fiona,' she said. 'The ulcer on her leg has healed up nicely, but she shouldn't be in that large old house alone unless someone has a key.'

'She has a family,' Fiona said, remembering fondly the ageing widow and her four daughters who visited regularly.

'I know, but what good are they if she's taken ill during the night, or she falls? She simply refuses to allow anyone to have a key.'

'I'll have a chat, of course,' Fiona said, 'but she isn't easily persuaded.'

'Is that the Mrs Hartnell I remember?' Stephen asked,

47

and again he directed his intense stare at Fiona. 'She had some daughters, I believe, all married; can they really still be in the district?'

'Daphne moved away, the others are still around and hardly changed at all,' Fiona said. *Careful*, she told herself, *or you're going to drop yourself right in it and you don't want awkward questions asked in front of the whole team.*

'She was a very independent woman,' Stephen said, 'quite dominant, but I guess she had to be, being left a widow when quite young, with a family.'

'We'll let you visit if we get a call,' James offered.

'I'd like to see her again, she was a very likeable woman who everyone admired. Certainly my father did when she became a patient of his at the County when she was about seventy.'

'Maybe you're just the person to go and see her then. Perhaps you can persuade her to at least let one of the neighbours have a key,' Meggie said.

'Better let Fiona see what she can do first.' He flashed a disarming smile her way and she was forced to lower her gaze in embarrassment. 'You make monthly visits to all your elderly I take it?' he asked James.

'Those we feel warrant it, though Dr Locke was our mainstay there. He knew everyone so well. It's our policy to let Fiona and Meggie keep a watchful eye. We've found that if a doctor suddenly calls on them out of the blue they tend to worry that there's something wrong which we're not telling them about. When Dr Locke made his house calls he used to quizz the young and middle-aged about anyone living alone in close proximity. We found it worked quite well so we hope as you're already familiar with some of your patients you can carry on similarly.'

'I'll do my best, though I can't believe I shall know that many after so long.'

Meggie brought up the case of Sue Pines next which led to a discussion about Patsy's suitability to deal with young mothers.

'She's really too young to advise them,' Meggie said decisively. 'They can't confide in her, they feel she's too inexperienced.'

'But how does she gain experience without doing the job?' Fiona questioned.

'Get married and have babies of her own?' Stephen suggested cryptically, then with a smile, 'Sorry—it's not my place to comment, but I believe you're talking about the young lady who I met when I first came in. Auburn hair, baby blue eyes, a moderately buxom figure with the same degree of vitality?'

'That's our Patsy,' Perry said. 'She does have a lot to learn, but isn't that why she's Fiona's assistant?'

'Perhaps Fiona is too lenient with her?' Brian Sandford said.

'I'm sure Fiona is doing her best. Patsy's sort aren't the easiest type of people to keep in line,' James said, rushing to her defence.

'I'm not qualified any more than Patsy, in that I don't have a family of my own,' Fiona said. She felt the warm rush of protection from James even if he was at the other end of the table. He alone knew that she was physically unable to bear children, and he knew that Fiona preferred to keep such an intimate matter to herself. 'She's taken and passed her course and I feel she's very capable, *but*—' she paused, not relishing the thought of being disloyal to Patsy, 'she's a bit—well—bouncy, but that's why the older patients like her. She's *very* good with them, and in time I'm sure she'll learn to be equally diplomatic with our mums.'

James steered the topic of discussion away from Patsy in favour of what help could be given to Sue Pines, and the meeting dragged on. At last it was brought to a close, but before they dispersed James drew attention to the closure of the primary school. Most of them had heard about it and were genuinely sorry. 'Fiona has a petition she hopes you'll all sign,' he added.

There was mixed reaction among the team. Dave, the social worker, didn't feel he could put his name to a petition if the cost of keeping the school open merely for sentimental reasons, as he put it, didn't warrant it.

'If it closes,' he said, 'the kids will get a chance to go to a modern school and transport will have to be provided for the parents without cars.'

'With all the new babies we have on our lists surely it's going to be needed in a couple of years' time?' Perry said. 'Hand it over, Fiona, I'll willingly sign.'

'Me too,' Brian said, 'even if I do send our two to a private school.'

'What about you, Stephen?' James asked. 'You have three youngsters.'

Stephen sat back in his chair and tucked his pen in his top pocket significantly. 'I'm not much of a petition signer. Only one of mine is at school and she's already settled in a small private school near my parents' home. It seemed the best idea as I'm not too sure of the future yet. In any case I don't suppose I'd consider Kenelm Primary.'

'It's always been a very good school. I went there, followed on to junior school and then went to Gorton grammar school,' Fiona contributed angrily. 'Even those who went to the secondary modern have done very well, one boy to Cambridge even.'

'I'm not disputing its academic record, Fiona, but the building is old—positively ancient, in fact—and to be honest I want something better for my children,' Stephen said. 'Wouldn't you, if you had a family?'

'What was good enough for me would be good enough for my children,' she answered shortly, packing up her belongings and pushing her chair back. 'Excuse me, James, I must get back to my office.'

'We'll do our best for your campaign, Fiona,' James consoled. 'I'll be happy to sign the petition, even though I doubt if it will carry much weight.'

'You've changed your tune quickly. I thought you said we had to be realistic.' She hurried away, more angry with herself now for picking on James. She left Lizzie's room, which doubled as a lecture room, on the wake of stifled atmosphere.

'Well, how did it go? Did they all sign?' Patsy asked eagerly as Fiona closed the office door with a louder than necessary thud.

'One or two, but they aren't all that interested. Doctors are too pious to put their names on a petition.'

'Mm . . . you do surprise me, Fiona. I thought they were all archangels where you were concerned.'

'*Oh!*' Fiona ran her hand over her hair in agitation. 'I didn't expect—well, yes, I did—I expected one hundred per cent support, but they all agree it's an old school, which I must admit it is. It would cost the earth to modernise it, cheaper to build a new one.'

'Perhaps we could raise funds to modernise it, then the council would *have* to keep it open,' Patsy said.

'Better still, raise funds for a new one. Must be some wealthy landowner in the area who would donate the land, especially if he's a fond grandfather—oh—what's the use of indulging in pipe-dreams?'

'Wealthy people send their kids to private schools, and Catholics have their own. *They* always seem to be able to raise money for new buildings—hey! What about our local church?'

'Kenelm Primary was the original church school when the little church was used. It was known as St Simeon's then, but that's going back to before my time *and* my grandparents' time. Now,' she added thoughtfully, 'they raised enough funds to build the new St Peter's church nearer to the new housing estate. What's to stop them building a new primary school?'

'Cor—wouldn't that be great! Something we'd thought up.'

'Hold your horses, Patsy. I expect it's been suggested before, and the idea thrown out. Just keep touting for names. We let the junior school go too easily, but they are old enough to travel on the school bus to Gorton even if it isn't the best solution, but five to eight-year-olds is a different matter.'

'I'll go to church on Sunday and take my petition with me,' Patsy promised, 'and perhaps some of the mums will like me better if they can see I'm trying to help them—that I'm on their side.'

'Don't overdo it, Patsy, but it does help if you show you *care* about the community.'

'Well, of course I do,' the younger girl protested. 'I hope I shall be one of the "mums" one of these days.'

Fiona smiled at Patsy's enthusiasm and they discussed the day's work, and the following day's visits.

'I'm due to visit the Catholic school this month so I'll go tomorrow morning. I dare not mention the closing of Kenelm, and I certainly can't take a petition because they'd soon find room in their own school for all the local five-year-olds if necessary, but I might glean a few ideas for fund-raising.'

Patsy was almost too enthusiastic for Fiona who was glad when she went home, leaving her in comparative peace to do some paperwork. She had managed to put the project out of her mind and settled down to her normal routine when a knock on the door heralded Stephen's arrival. His large masculine frame seemed to fill the open doorway as he hesitated on the threshold.

'Can I come in?'

'Of course,' she managed to answer civilly, 'though I shall be off shortly.'

He closed the door and advanced slowly towards her desk. 'I suspect a lot of Dr Locke's patients are suddenly agreeable to seeing one of his longer-standing colleagues. There were quite a few cancellations this evening so I had a very short surgery, but I'll stay in case of emergencies.'

'They'll soon get used to you. When Perry first came everyone said he was much too young and handsome to be a good doctor, but now he's the most popular, after Dr Locke.'

'I . . . I'm sorry about the petition, Fiona. It isn't like you to get involved in such a thing, unless you've changed a hell of a lot.'

'I expect we've all changed, but my job is in the community, and I do care about seeing the demise of so many old traditional things.'

'I can go along with that, but most young parents do want the very best, the most up-to-date for their kids and you have to admit, Fiona, that Kenelm Primary had its day as St Simeon's.'

'There wouldn't be any need for a petition, Stephen, if there were to be a replacement. My "mums" want a local school for their five-year-olds and if Kenelm goes there'll only be the Catholic school, and one private kindergarten which doesn't have a favourable reputation. A petition of names might sway the balance at this early stage, and you have children not yet at school . . .'

'As James Coudray says, we have to be realistic.'

'It'll be too late to be realistic when Kenelm closes down.'

'You've turned into something of a fighter, Fiona.'

'I'm older, and maybe have things in their right perspective,' she muttered.

There was a momentary pause. Fiona wished Stephen would go away—right away, where she'd never see him again—but, oh, how she loved him still—if only it weren't such a painful emotion!

'Fiona—I'm trying to understand you. It was a shock to come here and find you back in this area. I heard you went to London to do your midwifery course and I presumed your marriage had taken you to some distant place. I refused to allow your name to be mentioned in my company; I only prayed for your happiness. I'm sorry if things didn't work out as you planned. I know you're known as Miss Meredith, but that need not necessarily mean what it implies. Forgive me for asking but it's important that I know from you—were you married —didn't it work?'

Looking up into the depths of his brown eyes made her breathless, and yet she wanted to blurt out the truth, but now she dared not tell him the real reason behind her decision to break off the engagement as he might suspect she would expect them to take up where they had left off. After all, he was a free man again.

'I never married, Stephen. That's all in the past and I don't wish to discuss it,' she said firmly.

'But you and James?'

'We have an understanding. We've become close over the years and I'm very fond of him. He and Dr Locke have been so good to me—especially when my parents retired and returned to Selkirk.'

'Is fondness a good enough basis for marriage?' he asked slowly.

Fiona went cold all over, and despised Stephen for having the audacity to pass judgment even if the same thought was seldom far from her own mind, thus causing a guilt complex.

'I know that for lots of women a father figure is an attraction,' he added softly.

'Don't try to analyse me, Stephen. What I do is my affair,' she retorted.

She lowered her gaze quickly to her report book, willing him to leave her.

'For old times' sake at least we can be civil to each other,' he said. 'We must be, or it will be impossible to work together.'

'Quite,' she agreed tetchily.

'I realise you would prefer that no one here should know about us, but you surely realise that there are still people around who remember, and my returning might create a fan to the flames.'

She glanced up at him. He might almost be pleased at the thought. Her expression indicated that he held the solution.

'No, Fiona, I'm not going to do a disappearing act simply for your benefit. I've been away for ten years and it's nice to be home again. I won't be an embarrassment to you, but for God's sake don't just use James Coudray —he's too nice a guy for that.'

'Get out of my office and mind your own business,' she

snapped angrily, standing up to face him.

With barely six inches of space between their faces, it was like watching her beloved photograph of him materialise and spring to life, shedding the past ten years. The amber flecks still muted the brown of his large almond-shaped eyes, his nose was straight with the shadow of a dent at the end, and his mouth still curved sensuously as a smile teased her temper, and then he strode arrogantly out of her office as requested.

Fiona sat down again and buried her face in her hands. How often had she visualised a reunion with him? A meeting in Gorton High Street perhaps when he was home visiting his parents, even though she knew that they had made annual journeys to Australia. A polite greeting, casual conversation which would end her craving for him once and for all, but reality had released all her secret longing and she knew that if Stephen stayed then she must go. But there was James. If she tried to run away, too much telling would have to be made public and all Fiona wanted was a quiet life. Oh, dear God, why did Stephen's wife have to die, and why did Dr Locke have to be taken ill just when she needed a confidant to free her of the past?

The persistent drizzle fell relentlessly for the next few days. Fiona filled her working schedule with visits and so avoided any further confrontations with Stephen. Even Patsy refrained from her usual non-stop chatter, perhaps sensing that Fiona had private worries.

She planned to visit Dr Locke in the nursing home where he had been moved at the weekend but James instantly suggested that they could lunch together in a country pub and then go on to see Dr Locke. Fiona felt she couldn't win, but on Sunday morning she woke to find the sun streaming through the curtains and it actually felt several degrees warmer. Spring brought renewed enthusiasm and hope, and with it extra energy to Cassie who brought Fiona's training shoes to her while she was breakfasting. Who could deny the soulful hazel eyes, head on one side and one ear flopped forward while the other remained alert for any unfamiliar sound.

'For goodness' sake, Cass,' she said through a mouthful of toast, 'let me get dressed first.'

She finished breakfast and washed up, then put on her emerald green track suit with the gold flashes, and her matching training shoes, while Cassie pawed and whined until at last Fiona opened the back door. She took the lead off the hook; though it wasn't needed in the forest, occasionally horse-riders excited Cassie and she might need to restrain her.

After locking up she set off, waving to Mr Hollis, the manager of the site supermarket, who was packing up milk crates outside the shop. 'I'll have my paper when I come back,' she called, and Cassie leapt over the five-barred gate while Fiona climbed over the stile into the woods. She quickly found a piece of twig to throw for Cassie and as she walked, and sometimes jogged, she breathed in the wonderful fresh spring air and the scent of pines, at the same time working off Cassie's surplus energy.

At the supermarket on her return Mr Hollis put the newspaper in Cassie's mouth, and without waiting for Fiona the golden retriever set off home proudly.

'You'll have that dog of yours visiting your patients for you before long, Fiona,' he said.

'That's an idea,' she began, 'use her for therapy—' A

screech of brakes sent her shooting outside with Mr
Hollis close behind.

Cassie was standing at Fiona's front gate looking back
at the stationary car with doggie contempt, her tail
drooping.

'Dogs should be on leashes,' the driver called, opening his window. There was a gasp. 'You!' Stephen
opened the door and got out in disbelief.

'Yes, *me*!' she replied steadily. 'Dogs don't need to be
on a lead as we're not on a public highway and, for your
information, in case you failed to notice the sign, there's
a five miles an hour speed limit through the site.'

'It's as well for you and your wretched animal that I
was travelling at a slow speed.'

'But more than five miles an hour, I bet.' She grinned,
not wanting to embark on another bitter disagreement.
'What are you doing here anyway?' she asked.

'Is the dog all right?' Mr Hollis enquired. 'Did you hit
her?'

'No—I have excellent brakes and usually look where
I'm going.' Stephen's eyes brightened as he faced Fiona
again. 'I could ask you what you're doing here?' he
added, glancing at Cassie who had sat down at the gate.

Fiona went to relieve her of the paper she was so
faithfully carrying. 'Good girl, Cass. Are you okay?'

'I didn't touch her, honestly,' Stephen said. 'Only
a whisker away, but the screech frightened her, I
expect.'

Mr Hollis returned to his shop, and Fiona opened her
gate. 'I live here,' she informed Stephen simply.

The expression which changed his face was one of
disbelief. 'Here? In a caravan? On a site?'

'Sixpenny Orchard has always been a lovely spot. The
farmer sold a small field as a caravan site, then more land

and gradually it's developed into quite a large holiday and residential complex.'

'But *you*—in a caravan?' Stephen repeated.

'A mobile home if you don't mind, and it's very comfortable. Main drainage and central heating, electricity and the telephone—you're welcome to see for yourself.' As soon as she'd said it she wished she had thought before speaking. What would people think? What would the gossips make of this reunion?

'I'd like to very much. I'll pull the car over.'

Fiona went through the gate and opened her back door to let Cassie in. It was going to be more difficult than she realised to remain aloof with Stephen. He quickly followed her in and closed the annexe door, then he bent down to fondle and talk to Cassie.

'You're quite young,' he cooed, 'too young to be the reason your mistress gave me my marching orders.'

Fiona pretended not to hear his remark as she filled the kettle, allowing the water to rush in noisily.

'Tea or coffee?' she called from the kitchen and he appeared at the doorway, filling the open space, a man of disillusionment, a man to be reckoned with.

'Whichever you're making, Fiona. I didn't realise caravans had conservatories,' he said, letting his gaze absorb every detail of what Fiona liked to think of as her sun room, which helped to keep the rest of her home warm and draught-proof, and was ideal to sit in to read or sew, or even to do her paperwork when she was busy.

'They don't,' she replied, 'I had mine built on—it makes a nice entrance.'

He surveyed the kitchen critically, and Fiona knew that he noticed the cooker, microwave, washing machine and fridge-freezer.

'I see you have everything,' he said.

'Hardly,' Fiona refuted, 'but I'm quite comfortable here, it's just the right size for me. Go through to the lounge, I'll bring the coffee in.'

'I can wait. I'm admiring your well-designed, bright kitchen.' He tapped the pine-wood table top, and slid into the bench seat. 'Gone quite continental, I see.'

Fiona shrugged. 'It was all the rage when I bought the unit, and it's convenient for me on my own.' She poured the measured milk and water into the china beakers she had placed on a small tray. 'But I'm not serving you with coffee here,' she continued edgily. 'My lounge is where I entertain guests.'

Stephen linked his fingers together comfortably on the table in front of him. He grinned devillishly the way he'd always done when he was trying to win her round to his way of thinking.

'You haven't changed that much, Fiona,' he said, studying her.

'Ten years isn't that long,' she retorted, and with head held high stalked past him into the spacious lounge. She switched on the imitation coals on the fire, but moments later Stephen was resting on the gateleg table staring out of the bay window at the view.

'I thought they liked to keep people out of the forest,' he said. 'There's a group of horse-riders coming along.'

Fiona explained how the project had grown over the last few years.

'It's a lovely spot,' she said, 'and the forest is all opened up to the public now.'

'I'd like my youngest to learn to horse-ride, the same as the older ones. We did a lot of it in Australia. I shall have to bring them up here.'

'I'll just briefly show you the rest,' she offered, 'if only to prove that it's not remotely like a caravan—not the sort you pull behind a car, that is.'

He nodded for her to proceed through the door at one end of the lounge which led to an oblong hallway where a glass front door was covered with dainty lace curtaining. On the opposite wall to the lounge a door stood open revealing a good sized double bedroom complete with vanitory unit and built-in wardrobes. He said little but his expression showed approval, also of the two smaller bedrooms and the bathroom.

'The size is deceptive,' he said. 'How long have you lived here?'

'Five years.'

'Is this where you intended to set up home and have a family?' Stephen looked down at her, his eyes suddenly cold, causing hers to burn uncomfortably. 'Or is this where you and James plan to make up for those lost years? What's taken you so long? You've evidently had something going between you for the past six years?'

'You don't need to sound so bitter, Stephen,' she managed to say. 'You married and had your family. James and me—well—we've always been good friends —and it progressed from there.'

His laugh was more of a sneer. 'Not exactly a passionate romance.'

'No,' she agreed haughtily, 'but sincere friendship and loyalty are longer lasting.'

'*You*—are telling *me* that?'

She flushed dark red knowing that, having come back to Kenelm and finding her here, he was bent on getting answers to questions. 'Please,' she whispered, 'the past is over and done with. Nothing can be gained by bringing it all up again.'

'On the contrary, Fiona. The gap would have gone on

widening if Martha hadn't died; but now I'm home again, and looking into your eyes I find I'm searching for some lost treasure. You've become a woman of mystery, Fiona, when the Fiona I loved was so open, unspoiled and honest. What really happened? And it's no good saying let sleeping dogs lie. Did you really believe that I could have avoided that other car that night? How could that crash have resulted in your sudden hatred of me? I'll never believe it was as cut and dried as that—there was more—*so* much more. It's tormented me for ten long years—isn't it time to come out with the truth? That while you were lying in hospital you fell in love with the young houseman at Ryelands General?'

Fiona stared blindly at him—the Stephen she had never ceased to love confronting her now with such unprecedented accusations.

CHAPTER FIVE

THE seconds on the clock ticked away unheeded as they stared at each other, Stephen demanding the truth, Fiona speechless with shock.

'You thought I didn't know, I suppose?' he barked sarcastically. 'Well, I'll tell you the truth—the thing that has haunted me all this time. I managed to get in to Ryelands past the night sister and all the staff you thought were protecting you. I was determined to make one last effort to plead forgiveness. I thought if I could see you alone I'd be successful in getting through to you. I got to the door and it was like being stabbed in the back—there you were with him, holding hands. *Fiona* —how could you?'

She covered her face with her hands, trying to remember the nightmare of those days in Ryelands. She heard the clink of china as he stirred his coffee, and her lounge almost echoed with vibration in the thick stillness. His gulps as he downed his coffee sounded ominous as she recalled the endless nights of weeping despite the sleeping pills Dr David Saunders had prescribed. It wasn't a bit like Stephen imagined. David had devoted his time to trying to help her forget the crash, little knowing the real cause of her distress. He was just a kind, caring young doctor. If Stephen had so readily jumped to conclusions how could he ever have really loved her as he had declared? *His* love had quickly turned to hate, so now there was no point in trying to convince him how wrong he was. The damage was irreparable.

'It all happened a long time ago,' she said solemnly. 'I've had to live with my mistakes, Stephen. As I told you before, I don't wish to discuss it.' She picked up her coffee and standing with her back to him sipped it slowly as the pain of deception seared her heart.

After a minute or so he replaced the beaker on the tray and came to stand in her shadow. He placed a forceful hand on her shoulder.

'I guess you were too young to be tied down, but I really thought nothing could *ever* have come between *us*.'

Fiona sighed. She didn't turn—it was so much easier to hedge and deceive without facing Stephen.

'What really came between us, Stephen, was mis-understandings,' she admitted softly.

He turned her round roughly, causing the remains of her coffee to slop dangerously.

'Then for God's sake let's get those misunderstand-ings out in the open,' he demanded, 'let's clear the air once and for all.'

She dared to raise her glance to meet his eyes, darkly savage with recriminations which had smouldered away for a decade. Was that how it had been? Or had their meeting again revived the past? His happiness had been snatched away recently and now he was vulnerable.

'It's—too—late,' she managed to say, licking a couple of droplets of coffee from her hand.

'Yes,' he agreed aggressively, then in a more subdued tone, 'yes, of course, there's James Coudray.' He took a few paces towards the door then looking directly at Fiona asked, 'What happened to the Ryelands romance —just for the record?'

She hesitated, hurt and confused, afraid that if she started talking she would reveal too much.

'Ryelands is all in the past and that's where it stays,' she replied without conviction.

He nodded. 'I see.' He shrugged. 'I must be off—I was called out to an elderly man with suspected prostate problems. I'll call back later in the day, but I must return to the surgery in case someone needs me.'

'The doctors usually take calls at home on Sundays.'

'So I believe, but there are a few things I need to familiarise myself with while I have the opportunity and it's a fair jaunt to Gorton and back. I'd probably no sooner get home than I'd have to turn round and come back here so I'm staying put for a couple of hours. Brian has gone to a seminar at the county hospital this morning so I'm covering for him, but I've told Mrs Carter to call me at home if she needs me. I like to see a case through, and if I decide to stay I need to get used to my patients as quickly as possible.'

He went through the kitchen and half way down the stone steps outside the back door he paused. 'You have a very nice little place here,' he said. 'Certainly a grand spot, but a bit isolated for a woman on her own. Aren't you scared? You used to be—of spiders, and the dark!' His face muscles relaxed with youthful memories.

'In the winter it can be a bit spooky when the holiday area is unused, but caravan owners are starting to come every weekend to get ready for the season, and I've always got the Hollis's. Mr Hollis manages the shop, and they have a double mobile unit like mine, my nearest neighbours, in fact, so I'm well looked after.'

'We'll probably meet again. I enjoyed riding in Australia. Becky, my eldest, is horse crazy so she'll be able to continue lessons here, and if we stay I can start the other two.'

'Then you'll need a good school,' she reminded him.

She suddenly found she was trying to hold on to him. The deep longing, suppressed with the passage of time, was eager to be released, and somehow the barriers were less of an obstacle than she'd imagined.

'Keep up the good fight, Fiona, but don't be too disappointed if you don't win,' he said. 'Bye now,' and he was gone.

Fiona returned to her lounge, tucked her feet beneath her on the settee and became lost in a dream world which she had promised herself was fading—until a week ago.

The name of Ryelands General in the west country held such poignant memories. When the full realisation of her injuries had been made known to her she had been relieved that she was in a hospital which neither she, Stephen, nor any of their respective families had much knowledge of. She had deemed it fortuitous that at the time of the accident Stephen's parents had been holidaying in the West Indies, so his father had not visited to ask questions. To be suddenly told at twenty-two years of age that your womanhood was less than complete had been the most cruel blow she had ever received. For no apparent reason she had felt guilty, and guilt had necessitated secrecy which had become of magnum proportions no matter how much her own parents had patiently reasoned that in time she would see things differently.

Many times she had told herself that being unable to bear children was an unsolicited fact, but not of paramount importance to one's happiness. Dear David Saunders had spent hours of patient reasoning all to no avail in the early days, and now with the arrival of Stephen she found that her barren useless body was more of a burden than she had reckoned with. She thought she had at last accepted the inevitable. She felt fortunate in that James had been so reassuring, but now the old wound was festering again. James was only agreeing that he didn't want a family to please her—to get her to the altar, but what if after they were married he should use this against her? Human nature was balanced on a frail link of trust and understanding! In a moment of frustration, anger, incompatibility, would it become a bone of contention between them?

Thoughts of marriage had begun to be a rainbow of romantic pleasure of late, but now dark clouds of un-certainty were casting deep shadows on her horizon and she felt as if she had been pushed back in time. But, she argued, this is a *new* time. You can't go back, you can't relive what has gone before, present and future are all that matters even if the situation changes, and didn't life change constantly? She was glad that up until now James had not insisted on an engagement, although he fre-quently mentioned a visit to London to the best Hatton Garden jewellers. A ring would be a positive gesture and a step nearer committing herself. Poor James. She was treating him badly, but now that Stephen was around —the telephone rang, and for a moment she stared at it, unable to move.

She knew it would be James, and it was.

'Hullo, I was just thinking about you,' she said lightly.

'Oh, good! That has to be significant.'

Wasn't she just too honest for her own good?

'Darling?' he pressed in a low, seductive tone. 'Some-times it's easier to say things over the telephone. Tell me what I want to hear—please?'

Fiona felt her nerves jangle, but she laughed a little too boldly. 'It's still morning, and I thought perhaps you'd changed your mind about a pub lunch,' she said.

'Nothing very romantic about a pub lunch, I agree,'

James said, 'but romantic interludes early in the day can be quite exciting when you're getting on a bit.'

'How you do go on about your age,' she teased.

'It's all right for you, you're still young and *very* desirable.'

But horribly incomplete, she thought, then pulled herself up sharply. She must stop feeling sorry for herself.

'Life's not the same once you've turned thirty,' she laughed.

'No, darling, it starts at forty, and wisdom is what it's all about—that's where we shall be so lucky—we've got that to build on.'

'Now you're getting too serious,' she quipped. 'Did you ring for a special reason?'

'It's always a special reason just to hear your voice, and it brings you close to me, but actually I've just had a call from Stephen asking me to meet him at the Centre.'

'Oh—I saw him earlier when I went to fetch my paper. He nearly ran Cass down. He was called out to see Mr Carter—something worse developed?'

'I've no idea, he didn't say, only that he wondered if I could spare a couple of hours for a chat this afternoon. As you know I'm very keen to have him join our team, so I hoped you'd understand?'

'You'd rather skip lunch?' she suggested, hiding the hope in her voice.

'Darling—I know this is an unforgivable thing to do, but I've arranged to meet Stephen in The Crown. Would you like to come along too?'

'No.' She hoped she didn't sound too decisive, but she was rather grateful for this intervention. 'I can always find things to do.'

'Dinner somewhere this evening then—we'll drive into Gorton. I'm sorry about visiting Dr Locke, but they've moved him to Sheldrake Lodge which is nearer. We could go one evening.'

'That's good. If he's at Sheldrake I'll have a bite to eat and visit him this afternoon. I would like to go, I feel I should.'

'Of course, darling. Please give my apologies, and I'll make a special effort to look in on my round tomorrow. He'll be glad to be closer to home.'

'That sounds like good news,' she said.

'I hope so—I'll pick you up around seven-thirty then, okay?'

Fiona agreed, and replaced the receiver with a sigh of relief, but she didn't have time to brood over events as she had to bath and change, prepare and eat a salad lunch before going to see her beloved Dr Locke.

The fact that he had been moved to Sheldrake, an exclusive nursing home in Kenelm, must surely mean that he was progressing satisfactorily, but when Fiona was shown into the large, airy room the sad, immobile figure in the bed stunned her. She was well used to visiting stroke victims, and was aware of the will most of them showed to improve, and regain speech and mobility, but Dr Locke looked extremely ill.

'Fiona, my dear, how good of you to come,' Mrs Locke greeted with a kiss. 'I'm afraid Esmond may not respond though. One day he seems to be listening and another day, like today, well—I have to keep looking to assure myself that he's breathing.'

'I was away on a course, Mrs Locke. It was a dreadful shock to come home and hear the news.'

'Shock is the appropriate word, my dear. That's what they call a stroke up north as you probably know. Poor darling, he showed no sign of being poorly—a little slower in getting up, that's all—it was as much of a shock to him and me as anyone else. James was most kind. Esmond would hate to think he had let the Centre down. I've been telling him that Stephen Radcliffe has come in as locum—oh, my dear Fiona—has that been quite dreadful for you?'

'We collided on my first day back. It was Stephen who told me that Dr Locke had been taken ill.'

'How is Stephen?—a widower now, of course. Has he changed much?'

'Not really—a little older like the rest of us, but surprisingly much the same.'

'Will his return make any difference to your plans, my dear?'

'Why should it?' Fiona said as convincingly as possible. 'We went our separate ways ten years ago.'

'But you can't just disregard what you had between you—and he is a free man now.'

'Oh, Mrs Locke,' Fiona breathed with an attempted nonchalant laugh, 'Stephen would never trust me now. He obviously thought I jilted him for someone else.'

'Wasn't that what you wanted him to think?'

'Ye-es. At the time I considered it was the fairest thing to do. If he'd known the truth he would have felt honour bound to marry me from a sense of duty, and he would have been denied children. It might have come between us. As it is, it was easier for him to accept if he'd lost me to another man.'

'And James?'

'He's taken it for granted that we're going to be married. I tried to tell him that I'd known Stephen years ago, but he also knew Stephen for a short time together at Bristol just before he emigrated. He'd even heard how Stephen was cruelly jilted, so I just couldn't bring myself to tell him it was me.'

'But surely, my dear, you'll have to be more explicit —before you get married?'

Fiona felt her chin tremble. How could she tell anyone that now, having met Stephen again, she could not go through with the proposed marriage to James? On the other hand she must in order to alienate herself from Stephen.

'I knew nothing about Stephen being a widower,' she said falteringly.

'Esmond wondered whether or not he should tell you, but when he didn't return home immediately it seemed pointless to rake up the past. It's good for us that he came home just at the right time.'

'But Dr Locke is going to be all right, isn't he?' Even as she spoke doubt accompanied each word.

Mrs Locke, a petite, bright little woman, spoke in a hushed voice. 'We can't be sure how much he hears. It's bad, Fiona.' She fought back tears bravely. 'He was always *going* to retire—"next" year, and when next year came he put it off because he loved his work, and was devoted to the people of Kenelm.'

'It's hard to imagine the practice without him.'

'James is ideally suited to be in command, and Stephen next in line, if he stays.'

Fiona gave a long drawn-out sigh. 'If he stays I shall have to go.'

'But James's job is here.'

Fiona was silent as she too fought her emotions. 'We'll just have to wait and see.' She moved over to the bed and took the elderly doctor's hand in hers. 'Come on, Dr Locke—fight—just as you've always told your patients to do. You *mustn't*—you *can't*—give in,' she whispered frantically. Did she really feel some response in his hand, or was it her imagination?

Fiona stayed a few minutes more, but memories and heartache affected her so deeply that she was glad to leave. By the time she reached her car her vision was totally blurred. Dear Dr Locke, the man in whom she had confided often in greater depth than to her own parents, the man who consoled, comforted, and advised, was lost to her now—probably for ever. She felt as if her world was collapsing around her as easily as a falling pack of cards. Her fingers groped clumsily between handkerchief and keys.

'Fiona—whatever is the matter?' The last person in the world she had expected or wanted to see was Stephen. Wasn't he supposed to be chatting to James?

'What are you doing here?' she blurted. 'Come to make sure that Dr Locke isn't going to get better?'

There was a long pause.

'Fiona—come on now, this isn't like you.'

'Like me? How would you know *what* I'm like?' She was angry, hurt and confused, and somehow there had to be an escape route for her personal grief. She laid her arm on the top of the car, rested her forehead on it and gave way to sobs of sadness for Dr Locke, as well as regret for her hurtful attitude to Stephen.

Stephen's arms around her gave her a feeling of warm shelter. Time ebbed backwards, she was carefree and young, and very much in love. Even though they had lived thousands of miles apart the years had strengthened that love. Through the tweed of his jacket Fiona could feel the physical energy of the man and she drew strength from him. 'I'm . . . I'm sorry—it's terribly upsetting to see Dr Locke so weak,' she said. 'So—so —defeated.'

His arms closed more securely as he turned her round, and with one finger he eased her chin up to face him.

'I do understand how you feel, Fiona. Dr Locke is and has been Kenelm, but he was overdue for retirement. Maybe it's not as bad as you think, though of course he won't be able to work full time again. Here at Sheldrake he'll get the best treatment; they specialise in stroke patients so we must all persuade him to fight back, and I'm sure he will.'

Fiona blew her nose and dried her eyes. 'I must look a mess,' she said.

'A sight for sore eyes,' he chided with an amused chuckle. 'Fiona—I know I can never take Dr Locke's place in the popularity poll, but James assures me that both Dr and Mrs Locke would like to have me as a member of the team. I didn't realise how glad I'd be to be back. I thought I'd just idle the weeks away while I searched for some new project to attack, but I *must* work, and my parents want me to stay. They're getting on, I can't deprive them of my children any longer.'

'Then you've decided to stay permanently?'

'Do you mind?'

'Why should I?' She tried desperately hard to sound indifferent.

'I don't want to cause you any embarrassment. There will be folk who'll remember, so it won't be easy for either of us, but it can be our secret. If we don't mention it then perhaps no one else will, and when you and James get married the past will soon be forgotten.' He suddenly bent and kissed her cheek. 'For old times' sake, my dear. Cheer up, in another week or two Dr Locke will be making a nuisance of himself checking up on all of us—you'll see.' He added a little pat of consolation on her shoulder and walked briskly across the tarmac drive to the front door of the nursing home.

Fiona sat in the driving seat feeling faint-hearted, and at the same time elated at his kiss. It was a few minutes before she could move off. In fact she watched Stephen in her mirror, waiting for his ring at the front door to be answered, and only when he had been invited inside did she start up her engine and back round before driving home.

She didn't want to go home. Stephen's chat with James hadn't lasted very long and she was afraid that James would be trying to contact her before the pre-arranged time, so she pulled into Kenelm's large land-scaped park and set off to walk with Cassie who was always ready to explore new territory. They didn't often come this way with the forest walks right on their doorstep, so Fiona kept Cassie on her lead until she had skirted the small boating lake and walked over the grassy hill to a more remote area. She tried to imagine what she would say to James later on. Was this the time to confess everything, or had Stephen done it for her? She knew that she should be straightforward now, before James heard it all from someone else, but if she once started talking she knew that she would have to tell him that she couldn't marry him, and the last thing she wanted to do was to hurt James.

She managed to walk off some of her turbulent anxiety and came to the conclusion that just because Dr Locke had been taken ill and a new doctor appointed in his place, it didn't mean that anything need change in her private life. The fact that Stephen Radcliffe was the new doctor was unfortunate, but she resolved to try to behave just as normal, as if everything was the same as before she went away on the course.

When she reached Forest View Chalet she fed Cassie who was quite ravenous, and then sat down with a much needed cup of tea before going to freshen up and change for her date with James. He, like Stephen, was always immaculately dressed and well-groomed, so she did her best to complement his perfections. The afternoon had been sunny and pleasantly mild, but now there was an evening chill so she changed her corded velvet suit for a jersey-wool dress in dark red. It had a dainty lace collar and cuffs, and although the style was simple it enhanced her slender figure. A red crystal pendant and matching ear-rings were all the jewellery she wore, and when she surveyed herself in the mirror she was satisfied with her appearance, including elephant grey court shoes and handbag, and short coney jacket.

It was unlike James to be late, but it was well past seven-thirty when she heard his car pull up outside. Cassie barked, not so much as a sign of her protection, but in eager anticipation of a walk with her favourite man. Fiona opened the door ready to greet James affably, but he took his time getting out of the car.

'We can be off then if you're ready,' he said, holding open the gate. She expected him to come in and check that her alarm system was set correctly before they left, also to make a fuss of Cassie which usually took precedence over everything else. Then she realised that he had been delayed and was concerned about punctuality wherever he had booked a table. She quickly glanced round, closed doors, left her lounge light on and settled Cassie in her basket before locking up.

'Were you delayed?' she asked brightly. 'But you weren't on call, were you?'

'No, Brian was back to take over from Stephen. I'm not that late, am I? The time went on, and there was lots to discuss with Stephen. It's all settled now, thank goodness, he's agreed to be our new partner. It'll be difficult for us all to get used to being without Dr Locke, but I'm confident that Stephen will be a great asset in the area.'

'I thought he hadn't made up his mind,' Fiona remarked casually.

'He knew I was keen to have him, and not to have uncertainty hanging over our heads, so he came to a fairly quick decision, one he feels is best for himself and his family.'

James pulled across the main dual carriageway and picked up speed rapidly in his grand Mercedes. It was his second love after Fiona, and the subject of much good-humoured banter, but tonight Fiona felt he was more compatible with his car than with her.

As the evening progressed he did relax a little, and responded to Fiona's efforts to be an especially good dining companion. They were in one of Gorton's best hotels where an old-fashioned trio of musicians played Palm Court type melodies, a fitting background to the tastes of the better class clientele who dined by candle-light in intimate reservation over a several course meal. Flickering shadows played tricks on Fiona as she tried to study James' expression. Was it tired lines which made him look tense, or was there really a hard, strained look about him? He chatted easily enough, deliberately avoiding talking shop, though they briefly discussed the closing of the primary school at Kenelm. She expressed her concern over Dr Locke too, but made no mention of the fact that she had met Stephen at the nursing home. It had been barely four o'clock so why had James indicated that his meeting with Stephen had run on longer that intended?

In the hotel lounge they sat side by side on a plush settee enjoying liqueurs with their coffee as they listened to the music, and it was almost eleven when James accompanied Fiona into her home.

'Another coffee?' she asked him, shrugging herself out of her jacket.

'Um . . . no, I don't think so, thanks, darling. We both have to be up early in the morning, so I'll say good night.'

He held her briefly, and kissed her gently. Tonight of all nights, when she had psyched herself up to reciprocate his amorous advances, he left her abruptly with a tension of ice in his wake.

CHAPTER SIX

FIONA couldn't imagine what she had done to upset James, except that she had gone to see Dr Locke by herself, but it was he who had put her off to meet Stephen at the pub, so she could hardly be blamed for that. Perhaps he was worried about the practice. Dr Locke, a gentle giant of a man, showed his strength in his calm appraisal of every situation, rarely losing his cool or ever showing signs of strain. He had the aptitude to pacify everyone around him and even in just the week Fiona had been back at work she sensed the atmosphere changing. She lay awake for over an hour thinking, wondering what the days ahead might bring. She resolved to continue her work as best she could, and to go on towards a deeper understanding with James, and, however hard it was, to try to forget that there had ever been anything between Stephen and herself. They were different people now from a decade ago.

As always, Monday morning was chaotic. She was in early but the telephone lines were buzzing continuously, and a queue of patients had formed at the reception desk.

Patsy arrived soon after Fiona. Normally she was not at her best on Monday mornings, any morning for that matter, but today she appeared wide awake and full of enthusiasm.

'Morning, Fiona,' she greeted cheerily. 'I went to church yesterday—you should have come too—everyone signed the petition.'

'Oh, Patsy,' Fiona held her forehead in dismay. 'You shouldn't have asked people without getting permission from the vicar first.'

'*All* right!' Patsy perched herself on the edge of Fiona's desk and pulled her tight skirt over her thick thighs. 'Keep your hair on! I *did* ask the vicar—on Saturday night at the disco.'

'The vicar was at the disco?'

'He looked in—mm . . . no, he stayed for quite a while now I come to think of it. I think he was checking up on us. Anyway,' she continued proudly, 'I got all the youngsters to sign, so naturally he asked what it was all about. He's been trying to think of a way to keep the school open. He's as concerned as everyone else. It's all going to be be brought up at the Church Council meeting.'

'Well done, Patsy. The more stir we create the more likely we are to at least get the closure delayed.'

'We ought to go through our registers and get some sort of figure of how many toddlers we have who will need school shortly.'

'That's a good idea. They've got a good play group at the church hall now, so they ought to progress to a nursery class for pre-school children. I think you're right, Patsy, it is the church we should be stirring up.'

The telephone rang, and the day's work began with a near hysterical Mrs Craven.

'I thought our Cathy had gone to stay with Anita,' she shouted down the line, 'but Anita has just telephoned to ask where she is.'

'All right, Mrs Craven—now keep calm, she's prob-ably stayed overnight with a friend. When did you last see her?'

'Friday teatime. She's been staying at Anita's all

week, and I suggested she came home for the weekend while Keith was off, but she said Anita had asked her to stay on for a few more days as Keith isn't all that confident with the baby yet.'

'How is Anita?'

'Her ankle is much better. She could easily manage without help now, but I thought it would keep Cathy occupied. I never thought she'd lie to me, Fiona. I dread to think what she might have been up to.'

'Let's hope nothing bad, Mrs Craven. Cathy has always seemed a sensible girl—has she changed of late?'

'We-ell,' Mrs Craven sobbed, 'it's the company she's got in with. Leather skirts, and pink and green hair—of course, her father gave her a right telling off when he was home on leave and saw her with a chalk-white face and black make-up. There was a bit of a rumpus last Wednesday evening before he returned to the airport, and Cathy went back to Anita's house. Now Anita says that she left them on Friday evening and none of us have seen her since.'

'I'll get in touch with our social worker, Dave. We'll find her, don't worry. Can you tell me who her friends are, and where they live?'

Mrs Craven was rather vague about Cathy's friends. They had always seemed such a respectable family—still were, of course, but it was a blow to their pride that Cathy couldn't get work. Fiona did her best to reassure Mrs Craven and then went in search of Dave whose office was next door to her own, but he wasn't there. She decided to go down to Reception to pick up any messages and look at the doctors' pad, and as she passed Dr Locke's surgery she noticed that already the name plate on the half open door had been changed to DR STEPHEN RADCLIFFE. Male voices could be heard from inside, and Fiona knocked and went in, knowing that James was with Stephen.

'Hullo, Fiona, some sort of crisis?' James greeted with a smile.

'Good morning,' Fiona acknowledged both men. 'A crisis I suppose for Mrs Craven. Cathy's gone missing.' She went on to explain the details as she knew them.

'Stephen and I were hoping to have a couple of hours before calls to go through a few details, but someone ought to visit Mrs Craven.'

'I'll go,' Stephen offered. 'Good chance to meet the rest of the family as I've already met Anita Boughton. Her ankle is a good excuse to call on her as well.'

'Dave isn't in yet, but I'll leave a message for him,' Fiona said. 'Mrs Craven doesn't seem to know much about Cathy's friends except that they're a bad lot.'

'Cathy is quite different from her sister, but I'm afraid that's due to the change in lifestyles and social habits. There isn't much work in the area and Satan is only too eager to find mischief for idle hands to do,' James said thoughtfully.

'We don't know that Cathy has got into mischief,' Fiona defended. 'She might be staying with a friend, and just been thoughtless, or even had one of her asthmatic attacks.'

'If she's never stayed away before that doesn't sound a very plausible excuse, my dear, but we'll give Cathy the benefit of the doubt. Everyone is innocent until proven guilty according to Fiona,' James said to Stephen with a smile.

Fiona smiled too. 'I don't believe in looking for trouble—it usually finds me quickly enough,' she said.

She left the two doctors, slightly embarrassed at the strange situation she found herself in. Stephen, the man she loved and should have married. James, the one with whom she expected to share her life, affectionately, but without true love. Did Stephen realise what a fortunate man he was to have had a happy marriage and children? He should be counting his blessings, she thought as she retraced her steps to her office, instead of seeking to find answers to questions from the past. The two men seemed to be hitting it off right from the start which was good from the work point of view, but not easy for Fiona to take. She recalled that James had been a bit off last evening and she had put it down to some difference of opinion between them, but now in the light of this morning's affability that seemed highly unlikely. She felt a cold shiver run through her despite the pleasant warm spring morning. She wanted to be loyal to James, but already even here at the Centre things didn't seem the same without the influence of dear Dr Locke, the man who was the father figure and much loved character of the local community.

Fiona decided to take herself farther afield this morning to visit the gypsies living up on the Barrow, as well as a new mother-to-be at a small-holding a mile or two up the hill who hadn't yet signed her pregnancy form.

The gypsies usually treated Fiona with reserved respect, but today they gathered together in a semi-circle as she drew up on the gravel. Trouble, she thought —hadn't she said that it usually found her? She unstrapped herself and got out of the car clutching her shoulder bag. They were very suspicious of official looking attaché cases.

'Hullo,' she greeted cheerfully, 'thought I'd just drop by to see if everyone is okay.'

One of the young women with a baby in her arms and a toddler clinging to her skirt stepped forward.

'We'm all right, Miss. No call for you to drive all this way.'

A sure sign that all was not well, Fiona decided.

'Well, now that I am here I may as well have a look at the children.' She noticed one or two of the men trying to hide their youngsters behind them. 'I had to pass on my way to Sykes Hill,' she explained. 'Why aren't Vicky and Graham at school?' No point in hedging with niceties. They were hiding something so it was best to show them that she knew.

'Not feeling well, Miss,' one of the men said, then added bluntly, 'We've heard they're going to close the school down.'

'If you don't send your children regularly you're giving them a good excuse to do so,' Fiona said. 'Right, now, who shall we start with? How are you, Vicky?'

The child, a five-year-old golden-haired girl, ran forward readily, quite used to Fiona from her school visits.

'Stuff for my head, Miss—teacher said not to come back till I was clean,' she divulged proudly.

'Oh, Mrs Luther, why didn't you come to the Centre and ask for the usual stuff?' Fiona said.

'Don't you cut our Vicky's hair off, Miss, don't you dare,' one of the older women said, brandishing her potato peeler towards Fiona.

'Come on now, Gran, when have I ever suggested doing such a thing?'

'They cut off my girlie's hair and I ain't never forgave 'em—never!'

'That was years ago, and Mrs Luther's hair doesn't seem to have suffered any harm. Mrs Luther, Dr Locke has told you to keep a supply of the stuff to keep your children's heads free from nits. You know it works.'

'But Dr Locke ain't there no more.'

'That doesn't mean that you can't have the same remedy that you always have—and that's no reason to keep the children home. You want them to be educated, don't you?'

In this encampment there were nearly a dozen young children under the age of eight. They were a good group of people, hard-working and honest, but sometimes misguided, and suspicious of the authorities. Fiona had built up a good rapport with them over the past few years while they had been allowed to camp on the Barrow; she had learnt how to be firm without creating a barrier. Now, she laughed and talked with each family in turn promising that the necessary prescription for Prioderm would be waiting for them at the health centre by late afternoon. It wasn't only the gypsies who would need it either, she thought, smiling to herself, though they always got the blame; there were several other sources from where it could have been started. She would need to bring her school visit forward a little. Before leaving the gypsies she managed to persuade those who could write to sign her petition, then she drove across the Barrow to a desolate hill-plain where she passed a few cottages before coming to an isolated small-holding.

The young couple who lived on Sykes Hill had received much criticism, and some admiration at their attempt to be self-sufficient from the land.

Fiona drew up near some outhouses, sending clucking chickens in all directions, and almost immediately a young man in baggy trousers, check shirt and gum-boots appeared at the door of the barn.

'Hullo,' Fiona called, trying not to panic at the obvious aggressive reception she was about to receive.

'Didn't you see the sign back at the road?' the man barked.

'I wasn't looking for one,' Fiona said getting out of her car, 'I'm looking for Mrs Abilene?'

'Who *are* you?' Before Fiona could reply to this rudely toned question the man went on, 'We don't allow cars of any sort up here. We're trying to survive on clean air, and we can do without your damned petrol fumes.'

'I . . . I'm very sorry . . . I didn't realise—actually —I'm the health visitor and I understand Mrs Abilene is pregnant?'

'So what? What the hell has that got to do with you?'

'She should have signed a form when she visited the health centre. It's important to have medical care right from the early stages, Mr Abilene.'

'That's your opinion and you keep it to yourself, Miss. We do everything the way nature intended and I'll look after my wife now, *and* when the time comes.'

'Isn't that going a little bit far?' Fiona dared to suggest. 'Couldn't I just have a word with your wife?'

The man's gaze moved towards the cottage and with a disgruntled shrug of his shoulders he nodded towards the door from where a small, attractive girl emerged.

'Hullo,' she called. 'Looking for me?'

Fiona introduced herself and explained who she was. 'Your name was given to me at the health centre in Kenelm. I understand you're pregnant, but you haven't signed the form.'

'Oh, that. Well, we thought we ought to be registered somewhere, especially me on account of the baby, but I don't need any help—strictly naturists—I'm going to have it at home and Owen is going to deliver me.'

'I . . . I see, but, I'm not sure that's allowed. You

should see a doctor, have a check-up and at least discuss it with him.'

'No need, Miss Meredith——' Owen Abilene snapped.

'Please call me Fiona, everyone does. I've lived around here for most of my life. What a marvellous spot you've found to enjoy Mother Earth at her best—except in mid-winter perhaps. Don't you find it a bit lonely?'

The girl shook her head. 'Big towns are such violent places. We're both townies, but we'd had enough. I bake bread, sew, and feed the chickens while Owen chops wood, and sows the seeds. An attempt at the good life I suppose, but we're happy. He's an artist as well so is always busy. I expect you think we ought to join the gypsies?'

'Good gracious, no, they move on from time to time and they live in caravans—not quite like mine—but modern enough. You've got a lovely cottage.'

'Come on in and have a look. I understand you have to check us out, but everything here will be just as sterile as in hospital. Probably more so, because we've only got our own germs to combat.'

'But surely, Mrs Abilene, just a few days in hospital to have the baby,' Fiona suggested kindly, 'give yourself a rest, let the doctors see that you and the baby are okay. You should be having one or two ante-natal tests you know.'

The young mother-to-be smiled at Fiona's pleading, but shook her head. 'All the tests and medical care in the world couldn't save Owen's mother when his brother was born, so we're adamant about leaving things to nature.'

Fiona knew that she would only do more harm than good if she tried to force the issue, so she admired all the work the couple had done in the cottage, appreciating their natural talents and love of arts and crafts before she left.

When she reached the Centre at lunch time she went to the canteen for coffee and found Perry there.

'Ah—you'll do,' she said. 'Prescription for Prioderm urgently required for the gypsies, and have you got Mrs Abilene at Sykes Hill on your list?'

'Mm . . . don't recall the name. I've certainly never visited anyone up there. Isn't that where that young couple are living the good life? Back to nature and all that?'

'In a manner of speaking, though not quite in the way you'd like to interpret it. They are trying to make a living from the land, and they're all for clean, unpolluted air and don't want to mix with people and germs. I got told off for taking my car right into the yard. Apparently there's a "no entry" sign at the gateway leading on to their land. The point is, Mrs Abilene came here to register, but she didn't sign a pregnancy form.'

'Who did she see? Someone at reception or one of us?' Perry asked.

'I haven't gone into that yet. I'll check with Doreen after lunch, but we must be prepared for trouble; she —*they*—insist the baby is to be born in their cottage without outside interference.'

Perry let out a low whistle. 'Mm, that makes things awkward, never come across such a request before.'

'Not a request, Perry, they're both adamant. Mr Abilene more so because his mother died when his brother was born, which he blames on to the medical care she had.'

'So you didn't get the form signed?'

'No, and I soon realised it was no use trying to

pressurise. I imagine that whoever she saw felt the same. I'll have a word with James, it's going to be tricky. I'd say she's about five months on.'

'Without so much as a blood test?'

'Yes—but I doubt if our grandmothers ever had any tests. Modern methods are not necessarily right for everyone, Perry.'

'But if something goes wrong *we're* expected to answer the cry for help and know exactly what to do without the patient's history?'

'I suppose that's how it worked in the old days.'

'You seem surprisingly sympathetic to their ideas.'

'It's my job to try to understand other people's points of view, and I do see theirs, except that I believe they're carrying things too far. I don't think we're going to get anywhere but we'll have to discuss it at the next meeting. Any news of Cathy?'

'Cathy? Cathy who?'

'Oh, never mind—she's probably turned up by now. Dr Radcliffe was going to visit Mrs Craven and I did leave a message for Dave.'

'Actually I've been out all morning, quite a busy round of house calls—and, you'll be pleased to hear, getting a lot of support for keeping the school open.'

Fiona stirred her coffee thoughtfully. 'Mm—maybe I over-reacted about that. I suppose a new primary school nearer the modern housing estates is what's really needed.'

'Who's been twisting your arm, turncoat!' Perry's eyes twinkled mischievously. 'Or is it James' tender persuasion?'

Fiona felt her cheeks burning uncomfortably. 'If anyone's a turncoat it's James,' she said ungraciously. 'I do agree that we need to be realistic, and the old St

Simeon's is positively ancient so it would be nice to aim for a brand new building.'

'Reach for the sky, eh? No harm in trying.' He ate his last mouthful of lemon meringue pie with obvious relish.

'Our Katie's cooking gets better and better,' he said. 'Why don't you have a proper lunch? It would save you cooking when you get home.'

'I do occasionally, but today I'm not that hungry. I over indulged yesterday.' She picked up her empty cup and saucer. 'I'll leave the details of the necessary prescription for the gypsies with Doreen on my way out. Will you sign it before you go off, please?'

'I'm not going off unless we get an emergency, so I'll be here all afternoon. You're in a hurry just when I'm in need of some female company.'

'Sorry, Perry. Another time maybe. I'm concerned about Cathy Craven, and I'm due a visit to Mrs Hartnell as well as an emergency school visit.'

Fiona knew Perry Linnell was watching her as she left the canteen. For once she could have done with some light-hearted chat, but there simply wasn't time.

Mrs Hartnell lived in a pleasant part of Kenelm, near the old church and school. Fiona always called it 'the pretty road' because the side of St Simeon's Church spanned the eastern length of it and opposite were some early 1900 houses, all with wide front gardens and neat wooden gates and fencing. Along the pavement, their blossom opening to the spring sunshine, were several flowering cherry trees, alternately white and pink so that at this time of year whichever side of the road you stood the opposite side was equally as colourful. The church grounds were resplendent with forsythia and magnolia trees, along with old pines reaching to the heavens.

Fiona left her car near the church entrance and walked
through the peaceful churchyard where the inscriptions
on some of the ancient headstones were unreadable.
The birds were singing and the tops of the tall trees
sighed as a gentle westerly breeze forced them to do a
fan dance. Dear old St Simeon's. The solitude of it made
her feel strangely empty with its locked oak doors
sheltered beneath the ivy-covered porchway. Ten years
ago she and Stephen had been planning to make their
vows in the cold stone church. Ten years ago, she
recalled, the church may have been as cold as any other
old building but it radiated a warmth from the love the
people of Kenelm shared. The new church a mile away
was of modern architecture and design, with lots of huge
clear glass windows which made it light and airy. If she
married James she visualised standing beside him at the
ultra modern altar, yet somehow she felt the sacred
reverence which she would need would be lacking.

She put the thought away with impatience, doubts of
ever marrying anyone in either church crowding out
visions of past or future intentions. The school, that
must be her personal project, and she wouldn't be
satisfied until new mums had a decent school for their
children to attend, whether it was St Simeon's
modernised, or a new building, even prefabricated
classrooms. Soon she would visit the manse and discuss it
with the vicar and his wife. She glanced across at the
garden of the manse which was separated from the
churchyard by tall iron railings. Bushes and shrubs hid
the railings somewhat, but as she walked along the
isolated path a movement attracted her attention. Someone visiting a grave she supposed, but then she heard a
weak voice—or was it a muffled cry? Quickly she turned
on to the side pathway and to her horror she found Cathy

Craven sitting against the railings gasping for breath, clutching an inhalant in her hand.

'Cathy!' she exclaimed, bending low. 'It's all right, don't panic. Come on now, slow—deep breaths . . . good . . . *good*.'

Cathy was unable to speak so Fiona concentrated on diaphragmatic breathing instructions. It was several minutes before Cathy's condition improved and as her breathing gradually became easier Fiona had difficulty in keeping in check the many questions that had sprung to mind.

Cathy was as white as a sheet. 'It's all right, Cathy,' Fiona whispered, 'it's all right, the worst is over now.'

Fiona noticed Cathy's grubby jeans and stained tee-shirt which proclaimed evidence by sight and smell that its wearer had recently been vomiting.

'We'll soon have you home,' Fiona soothed, but Cathy gripped her hand, gasping, 'No, *no*!—I can't—go—home.'

'It'll be all right, Cathy, just calm down,' but even as she spoke her gaze fell on suspicious-looking canisters lying all around the shrubs and bushes. Glue-sniffers had been having a party. Cathy, a glue-sniffer!

CHAPTER SEVEN

FIONA recalled the local paper's headlines on several occasions in recent months—GLUE-SNIFFERS ON THE RAMPAGE IN CHURCHYARD. It had been assumed that a group of youngsters from Gorton or some other nearby town had chosen the grounds of the old St Simeon's to experiment, after which several grave-stones had been vandalised, crosses and vases smashed. Fiona realised with dismay that the culprits might well come from nearer home. She felt anger as well as disappointment at the sacrilege in this remote corner of the churchyard.

'I'm going to take you into Gorton hospital, Cathy,' Fiona said decisively, 'but first we'll go and ask the vicar to let your mother know you're all right.'

Cathy allowed herself to be helped up on to her feet, and Fiona supported her as she guided her to the main pathway and gate which led into the vicarage garden. When they reached the gracious old house she rang the bell impatiently, and it seemed an age before two shadows appeared inside the front door. Voices could be heard too, and Fiona held on to Cathy firmly, suspecting that any minute the young seventeen-year-old might make a dash for it, back to her unsavoury friends.

Slowly the door opened as the vicar still continued his conversation with his visitor who, Fiona was surprised to see, was Stephen.

'Cathy's had an asthmatic attack,' Fiona said hurriedly, though without panic, omitting any words of

greeting. 'I'm going to take her into Gorton. Could you
please telephone Mrs Craven, Mr Richardson?'

'Bring her inside, my dear.'

At once Mr Richardson, the vicar, a tall fresh-faced
man in his late forties, took Cathy's arm and she seemed
grateful for a fatherly chest to rest against while tears fell
readily down her cheeks.

Stephen looked at Fiona, knowing by her expression
that there was something beside Cathy's asthma which
was troubling her.

'What is it?' he asked in a low voice.

'Glue-sniffing,' she said solemnly. 'There's every evidence of it in the churchyard. We've known it was going
on for a few months but no one's ever been caught. I
found Cathy hiding among the bushes surrounded by the
canisters and other rubbish. It's possible she hasn't, but
on the other hand it's just the kind of thing which would
bring on an attack of asthma.'

'I'll give her the once over then I'll take her into
Gorton myself while you fetch her mother,' Stephen
commanded. 'The reason I'm here was to seek the
vicar's help in finding Cathy or her friends. Mrs Craven
is beside herself with worry, you'll probably be more of a
comfort to her at present than me as we've only just
met.'

'The police—the Centre,' Fiona suggested.

'I'm sure that Mr Richardson will be only too pleased
to phone around. Cathy needs a check-up, and she'll
likely need familiar faces around her, so off you go and
fetch her mum.'

Fiona wasn't sorry to have the responsibility shared
and when she reached the Cravens' home Anita let her
in.

'I just can't pacify Mum,' she sobbed to Fiona. 'She

would insist on getting through to Dad, he'll be furious.'

'Then tell her quickly that Cathy is okay. She's had an asthmatic attack and Dr Radcliffe has taken her into Gorton General for a thorough check-up.'

Fiona could hear Mrs Craven's hysterical voice coming from the kitchen where she was using the telephone extension, and a cry of relief was evident as Anita gave her mother the news. A few minutes later Mrs Craven came into the hall.

'Oh, Fiona, this is all my fault. I should have taken more interest in those awful friends of hers. Did she say where she's been staying?'

'No, but we'd best not go into that for the present. She's had a nasty attack, and she's frightened.'

Fiona did her best to console the distraught woman who talked non-stop all the way to the hospital.

The circumstances were a little difficult, Mr Craven being away from home most of the time as he was a flight controller at Heathrow Airport. They had come to live in Kenelm to get away from London and to settle in more rural surroundings in readiness for his retirement in a few years' time.

Fiona listened patiently, knowing how hard it was for a woman who had to shoulder the responsibilities of bringing up a teenage daughter single-handed, and the added pressures when Mr Craven came home. Mrs Craven talked of the stress of trying to keep the peace.

'Seven years' difference between the two girls is too long,' she declared. 'There was a boy in between, but he died at the age of two from a rare tumour.' She sighed emotionally. 'It's no use saying that Christopher's living and dying didn't affect us—it did, but . . . Cathy made it up to us. She's not a bad girl, Fiona, it's just this waste of time. She's become idle during this past year and it's now she needs her father. Anita was different. She suffered too, losing her baby brother, but then having Cathy,' she shrugged, 'Anita always seemed more grown up.'

'We're all different, Mrs Craven, and these days the temptations and social behaviour is vastly different even from ten years ago.'

They reached the hospital and at Reception were told to go up to the first floor where they found that Cathy had been admitted. Stephen had left, it seemed, and a welfare worker was waiting to talk to Mrs Craven and Cathy.

Fiona decided it was best to keep a low profile but Jean, the welfare worker, took her to one side.

'Cathy has told me that she was persuaded to spend the weekend with some youngsters who are squatting in a derelict house somewhere. Do you think she's telling the truth?'

'Most probably. She was very frightened by this asthmatic attack, she's been so much better recently, but in the vicinity where I found her there was evidence of glue-sniffing.'

'So Dr Radcliffe reported. They've decided to hospitalise her for forty-eight hours, and let's hope that it was a one-off experiment. Will you keep in touch, Fiona? She knows you and won't want to be counselled by a lot of strange people. Has your social worker dealt with the family at all?'

'No—there's never been any cause. I know Cathy from my school visits, and her elder sister is one of my mums with a five-month-old baby. I know all the family except Mr Craven.'

'Good, then we'll be in touch. Stay if you like, but there's a lot of sorting out to be done before we can send her home.'

'I'll either ring or come to see her tomorrow. She has her mum now so there's no point in my hanging around.'

As Fiona walked through the corridor of the large modern hospital she experienced a fleeting desire to go back to general nursing, or midwifery. Visiting the hospital had never affected her before, and she couldn't imagine why she felt this strange need at this moment. She tried to shrug it off as she walked across the vast car-park, and when she glanced up to see Stephen waiting by her car she realised the hidden implications. Subconsciously she was trying to turn the clock back. With the return of Stephen to Kenelm it seemed a natural evolvement to imagine them both working together in a busy hospital.

He smiled warmly as she approached. 'I expect Cathy is pleased that it was you who found her,' he said gently.

Fiona made a face. 'For Mrs Craven's sake I'm glad someone did, but I can't imagine what she was doing in the churchyard.'

'She's been staying in a squat with some of her old school friends. When the asthma started acting up they got scared and sent her packing, but she was too frightened to go home. She confided in me about the glue-sniffing. Just wanted to experiment and the feeling of euphoria made her want to continue—until she vomited.'

'Poor Cathy——'

'Come on, you look as if a cup of tea would buck you up. Let's go in my car and we'll come back for yours later.'

'I ought to get back to report to James.'

'I've already done that. Cup of tea—doctor's orders?'

The old magic persuasion worked and Fiona gave up trying to kick against it. She assumed he would take her to one of the quaint tea-shops in Gorton. It was a shadowy expectation in the back of her mind as they discussed Cathy's problems, and before she could comprehend his intentions, Fiona realised with extreme annoyance that he had driven to his parents' home.

'Stephen—*no*—I . . . I'm on duty. I didn't want to come *here*!' She knew it sounded ungrateful but the sight of his home turned her emotions to ashes, bringing back forgotten memories, taunting her with possibilities for the future—no—there could be no future with Stephen, however much her heart craved for it.

'Well, you're here now, so that's *it*!' he replied crisply. As they drew up in front of the huge oak door he unstrapped his belt and turned to look at her. 'Mother says you used to visit, then you suddenly stopped. Whatever went wrong between us, *they* still loved you dearly and were dreadfully hurt.'

Fiona felt a lump close her throat. This was unforgivable of him. Why couldn't he simply leave the past in the archives of family history? It was of little interest to anyone now. The present situation was strain enough, and she had to force herself to go on with the farce of loving James when all the time her passion was welling over for Stephen. Unanswered questions, unanswerable questions—would he never let go?

'I know they'll be delighted to see you. I'm sorry you can't meet my children,' he went on, 'they won't be back until later.'

He helped her out of the car. A part of her wanted to be stubborn, but when Stephen's father pulled alongside in his car she didn't have much choice but to fall in with Stephen's scheming.

'Fiona, my dear, this is a pleasant surprise.' Mr Radcliffe senior was a distinguished-looking gentleman, tall and well-built, and in spite of his years had a fine head of dark hair, modified by some attractive slate-grey in the neatly groomed waves. Fiona thought he appeared to be slimmer as he stood beside his son, but they were alike in almost every other respect.

'I've brought her for a much needed cup of tea, now that Kenelm's runaway teenager has been settled in.' Stephen placed his hands on Fiona's shoulders and guided her forward as he explained that he'd seen his father at the hospital. 'Dad said that he was coming home and that Mum would definitely have the kettle on at this time of day.'

'So what are you all doing standing about out there?' Mrs Radcliffe opened the front door and with arms outstretched came forward eagerly to hug and kiss Fiona, whose stiff upper lip quivered and finally lost control. This was *awful*! How could Stephen put her into such a situation?

'Go and powder your nose, Fiona,' Mrs Radcliffe whispered, 'then come on down to the sun-lounge where tea is all prepared.'

Fiona was grateful for a few moments alone in this dear, sweet place she had once thought of as her second home, then, completely composed she walked casually through the sitting-room at the back of the house to the sun-lounge.

'What a pity the children aren't here, but you'll all meet soon I'm sure.' Mrs Radcliffe, a very elegant and yet homely woman, poured tea from the silver teapot into dainty china cups, and with a warm smile handed Fiona a cup.

Fiona wished she didn't like them all so much, but neither time nor change could diminish the wonderful family relationship they had all shared in the past.

The men discussed Cathy's problems at length.

'It's a growing menace,' Stephen's father said. 'So few jobs for school-leavers, time to search for excitement in drink, drugs or glue-sniffing. Stephen tells me this young girl comes from a good home, and seems very intelligent.'

'She is, and the family is a decent one. Cathy left school with one or two O levels which aren't a great deal of use to her. She wanted to do nursing, but she didn't have sufficient passes and there were no vacancies locally for an auxilliary. She's a little indecisive about what she wants to do, but how do any of us know what we really want to do when we've never actually tried the work? It's a shame because according to her mother she lost quite a bit of schooling in her primary and infant school days because of her asthma. Whether it was the move here from London, or she grew out of it we don't know, but she has been better since I've known them,' Fiona said. 'Again, because of her condition she's probably been a bit pampered, but that's only natural being the youngest.'

'It is difficult for young people, and all we can do is to bring home to them and their parents the dangers of these unpleasant addictions,' Mr Radcliffe said forcefully. 'They're afraid to say no, they don't want to be different from their friends or be thought of as "chicken".'

Fiona was pressed to eating sandwiches and cake with her cup of tea, and each time she tried to make her excuses Stephen reminded her that she was dependent upon him. 'I have okayed it with James,' he assured her with a mischievous grin.

'I'm not answerable to James,' she said. 'I have quite a heavy work load, and Patsy will wonder where I am.'

'Well you can't go until I agree to take you,' he retorted.

'Stop teasing, Stephen.' Mrs Radcliffe playfully smacked her son's knee. 'Come and see us again, Fiona dear, like you used to do. We've missed you, haven't we, Adrian?'

Mr Radcliffe glanced uneasily from his wife to Fiona.

'Of course we have, and Fiona knows that, but we must remember she has a life of her own, and I'm delighted that you and James Coudray—well—if the rumour is true,' he said to Fiona with raised, questioning eyebrows.

'James and I get along extremely well, he's a kind, understanding man and we've grown fond of each other, but——' the words tumbled out with ease, she could hardly believe they were coming from her mouth; if only she could reveal her deepest heartfelt desires! 'We haven't come to any long term commitments or made any plans,' she went on. 'I suppose when you get to our respective ages it isn't easy to give up your independence.'

She ought to have made it clear to them that there was an understanding between her and James otherwise they might think that she was making a play for Stephen. She wasn't used to giving false impressions; lying wasn't easy, and yet, eleven years ago hadn't she done just that with extreme feasibility?

She was glad to leave, though also content at having visited Stephen's parents again after so long, and she and Stephen travelled back to the hospital in comparative silence for the first few minutes. Stephen's jaw was set in a hard line and then he suddenly snapped out angrily, 'Kind? Understanding? Fond of each other? For God's sake, Fiona, you're considering marrying the man. Do you really expect that to be a good foundation to build the rest of your lives on?'

'I really don't think it has anything to do with you,' she replied bitterly. 'I didn't ask to be taken to your home and quizzed about my private life.'

'But your life won't be very private if you marry James Coudray.'

'It still isn't anything to do with you.'

'Is that what was wrong eleven years ago? Didn't I come over as kind and understanding after the crash? Was there something you wanted me to say or do that I didn't?'

'Leave the past out of it. What happened, happened, and I didn't blame you, whatever you may think.'

'*Think!* You didn't give me the chance to get at the truth, or to find out what *you* thought. Have a heart, Fiona, I thought we knew one another as well as any two people could. In the end I had to give in, and came to the conclusion that I didn't know you at all.'

'All right,' she yelled emotionally, 'so you formed your conclusion, leave it at that. You didn't know me, you still don't, so stop trying to rake it all up again.'

They were approaching the hospital, turning on to the complicated system of lanes and roundabouts which led into the car-park, and Stephen became tight-lipped.

She didn't want to fight him, but she knew she must, it was the only way or she would end up making a full confession and she didn't want his pity. But Stephen's pity was for James, she realised, as he mumbled, 'Poor James.'

It was cruel of him, and only served to make her determined to respond to James in a loving intimate way. When he jammed his brakes on so hard that she felt her body strain against her belt, she released it in a flurry of ill-temper.

'Don't be so damned pious,' she said angrily, 'and don't *ever* do this to me again. Remember that I was only civil because your parents have always treated me with the utmost respect and kindness.'

'*Kind!*' he growled, grabbing her wrist fiercely. 'Do you only measure in *kind*ness? Whatever happened to good old-fashioned love? Where did it all go, Fiona? To that good looking smoothie at Ryelands Hospital? And what did you get in return—just kindness?'

Fiona couldn't bear the jeer in his tone, it was so unlike the Stephen she remembered. She had experienced bitterness for the way fate had changed the course of her life, but she had never felt bitter towards Stephen. Now she knew that he had built up a great wall of contemptuous hatred against her. Had coming back to Kenelm meant that he intended to go on building it higher and stronger? Surely a good marriage and children should have helped such a barrier to crumble? She tugged to gain her freedom, but Stephen held on relentlessly.

'I can understand your hatred of everyone since losing your wife,' she said slowly, 'but trying to erase the past eleven years will only add to your despair, Stephen. We're different people now, and you have everything to work for, the future and stability for your children.'

She had succeeded in touching an exposed nerve. He dropped her wrist and sat tapping his forehead as she got out of the car and into her own. She didn't dare to look his way again or she was in danger of returning to his side to offer him comfort, and such an act might well result in her own humiliation.

It was well past five o'clock and the traffic towards

Kenelm heavy. She couldn't face James now, not tonight, and probably he'd have made a start on evening surgery. She would call in and see Mrs Hartnell though. Over a cup of tea the old lady's wise counsel would help to soothe Fiona's churning stomach.

Just one glimpse of spring fever in blossom in 'the pretty road' made her feel less fraught, and when Mrs Hartnell opened the door it was like being greeted by one's favourite grandmother.

'Fiona—you must have heard the kettle whistle! Come along, my dear, you look a bit pale.'

'I'm fine, Mrs Hartnell, and as I was passing I thought I'd pop in to see how you are.'

'Getting older, but wiser too, I suspect. I know why you've come, Fiona. Meggie is very good at her job, my leg has healed beautifully, but she does go on about my being here alone. Well, I *want* to stay here on my own. I've brought up a family and truth to tell it's nice to be able to please myself when I get up and when I go to bed, when I eat; I don't have to worry about anyone but myself. Now, I suppose you'll think I'm selfish?'

'Not at all, Mrs Hartnell. You deserve to be able to please yourself. You're not the kind of person to get depressed so I don't worry about you unduly, but if at any time you feel lonely you know you can always telephone me.'

'Bless your heart, Fiona, you're a good girl, but I like my own company and as long as I have my eyesight I can always knit or sew. I like to read too but my mother brought us up to only read on Sundays. On a working day it was considered such a waste of time.' She chuckled as she poured tea into pretty white cups bordered with a fine gold design. 'I bet you think that's nonsense?'

Fiona laughed too. 'Not at all. I've heard my own parents tell a similar story.'

'I expect you're glad you stayed here in Kenelm now that Stephen is back?'

'I think it might have been kinder of fate to lure me to some other town to work, Mrs Hartnell.'

'Fiona, don't let happiness slip from under your nose. Dr Coudray, is a nice, genuine man, but—' she shook her head solemnly, 'you and Stephen were always right for each other.'

'I expect there's a lot of things not quite as you saw them—and it's all so long ago now, it's best forgotten.'

Mrs Hartnell ran her work-worn finger round the edge of her saucer. 'I can only say to you what I'm always telling my girls—when you have a grievance sit down over a nice cup of tea and talk it out. It's no use talking to other people, you're the ones who know how you feel and you have to make sure that you each know how the other feels too. A little compromise, and total un-selfishness, and *anything* can be resolved.' She looked at Fiona directly. 'I'm not really as wise as I'm making myself out to be, but I do have four daughters, all happily married though I'm quite sure they've had their ups and downs.'

'You can be very proud of your family, and they do care about you and visit regularly, but—well—have you ever thought of letting one of them have a key—just in case of emergency? Supposing you locked yourself out in the garden for instance?' Fiona expertly channelled the conversation to the subject she'd come to discuss, but the elderly widow only laughed.

'A nice try, my dear, and I expect one day something will happen to force me into taking precautions, but I'm not quite ready yet to have people, even my own girls, barging in on me when I'm enjoying some nice music or getting on with some job or other.' She leaned forward and patted Fiona's arm. 'You start thinking about yourself—never mind me. I'm on the telephone, and I'm only seventy-six, maybe I'll give in gracefully when I get into my eighties, but independence is something to be valued—at *my* time of life, not yours. You're still young enough to put the past behind you and start again. You're in your prime and should be enjoying sharing your life with your man.'

CHAPTER EIGHT

Fiona drove back to the Centre with mixed feelings. Mrs Hartnell was a dear, and probably right about a great number of things except that she didn't know that Fiona's body was well past its prime. No matter what she and Stephen or she and James felt for each other, nothing could alter the fact that she wasn't a complete woman.

Glancing at her watch Fiona realised that surgeries would be over, and probably everyone gone home, but she found Doreen still behind the reception desk.

'One or two messages for you, Fiona, but nothing that Patsy couldn't handle. Had a grim day? You look washed out.'

Fiona smiled. 'I've known worse. At least we found Cathy.'

'Yes, that was a stroke of luck, though I can't believe she'd have anything to do with vandalising the church-yard.'

'None of the youngsters seem capable of such dreadful things when they're behaving normally. That's the sad part of it, they not only abuse themselves but everyone and everything around them. Once they're under the influence of these various addictions they just don't know what they're doing. It's dangerous for all of them, but for Cathy more so because of her asthma. She'll have to learn to say "no" or she'll destroy herself.'

'Aren't you glad you haven't got any kids? At least Cassie hasn't got any hang-ups.'

Fiona managed a responsive laugh with Doreen before hurrying up the stairs to her office, and almost at once James joined her.

'Everything sorted out, Fiona?' Was she imagining it or was there an edge to his tone?

'I don't know about that, James. Cathy Craven is going to need our help and support for quite a long time.'

'Shouldn't that be her parents' job?'

'A joint effort, I hope.' Fiona glanced with surprise at the unexpected reaction from James. A reminder of Dr Locke and his involvement with every family in Kenelm made Fiona's blood run cold. The changes were happening before anyone had time to readjust. Dr Locke would have gone to see Cathy, spent hours if need be with Mrs Craven, but Stephen had done his best to help, she remembered. It was well-known that some GPs weren't as helpful in such cases as they might have been. Perhaps it was through lack of knowledge, or the lack of time to get to the root of family troubles which were all too often the cause of youngsters turning to drugs, but some GPs were accused of being openly hostile. Fiona hoped Kenelm's health centre was going to be a place where at least some effort to help would always be maintained.

'Going home to put your feet up?' James asked.

'That's the best idea I've heard all day,' Fiona responded with a reticent smile.

'Laura has asked to be excused clinic duty tomorrow.'

'Oh? Isn't she well?'

'Some personal problem to deal with I think, so Perry has agreed to stand in for her. She's not sure whether she'll be able to make the weekly practice meeting on Wednesday afternoon.'

'We must discuss the problem of Mrs Abilene and her wanting to have her baby at home, James. She won't sign a pregnancy form, or her husband won't let her.'

'We can't let her have it at home.'

'Having visited them, James, I really don't see how we can prevent it.'

James sighed. 'They'll have to be persuaded. We'll talk it over on Wednesday.' He turned to go and Fiona was aware of his coolness towards her. Now, she thought impatiently, at a time when she needed to be mastered he was letting her down. She wasn't really sorry though that he wasn't making demands. After being with Stephen and the harassments of the day Fiona was very grateful for being able to go home and be on her own. How well she understood Mrs Hartnell.

She took Cassie for a quick run in the forest before she fed her, and then she sat down to enjoy her meal in peace, but as darkness shrouded the forest outside a cloak of loneliness enveloped her.

After a few hours' sleep she was awake before dawn. She could hear the deer munching at her rose bushes through the wire fence, and pulling back the curtain she could just make out their luminous eyes as they became alert to the slightest movement. She strained to watch them, a family of about seven, some drinking at the horses' water trough near the gate. She supposed she ought to switch the lights on to scare them away, but they were such lovely creatures she didn't have the heart. The chill of early morning made her shiver, and then a warmer thought of having someone one day to share sleepless hours of watching the deer at sunrise sent her happily to the kitchen to make tea. She realised it was a senseless thing to do, but the tea warmed her, and she checked that her alarm was set at the correct time before settling down to dreamy unconsciousness.

*   *   *

Fiona was sitting at her desk later sorting through messages when Patsy arrived.

'Morning,' the younger girl greeted, 'you're in early.'

'It's clinic day, and I feel I should visit Mrs Craven and Cathy this morning so perhaps we can reduce our visits today to the absolute minimum of necessity.'

Patsy pulled up a chair at the end of Fiona's desk and presented a few files to her, but Fiona realised that the younger girl was not her usual effervescent self as she was occupied with her own thoughts.

Fiona sat watching her colleague for a few seconds.

'A problem, Patsy?' she queried gently. 'Private, personal, or work?'

Patsy blinked wriggled her well-padded bottom to a more comfortable position on the chair and leaned forward with her elbows on the top file.

'Is Cathy all right?' she asked solemnly.

'Mm . . . yes, more scared than anything. Her shady friends turned her out of the squat when she had an asthmatic attack.'

'That was a mean thing to do.'

'They were probably terrified.'

'And they're not shady characters at all,' Patsy defended.

Fiona paused. 'No, I'm sure you're right, but how do you describe people who break into someone else's house and take it over? Cathy is a bright, intelligent girl and was well behaved until she met those people.'

'They were all at the disco on that Saturday evening. They seemed like good fun, and I don't think Cathy really wanted to go off with them but they persuaded her to go on to somewhere else.'

'The churchyard you think?'

Patsy nodded. 'I feel as if I should have tried to stop them. After all that's partly our job, isn't it?'

'We can't do much to stop them if they've made up their minds to indulge in such activities, but we can listen, and respond when they get into difficulties. I shall have to make school visits my next priority. We've been lucky in Kenelm up until now, with only minor incidents to deal with, but now that the area is growing, social habits and behaviour are changing, so we must get in quickly. I'll arrange a talk at the local schools as soon as possible.'

During the next hour they decided on visits, took telephone calls and dealt with messages, and then Fiona left the Centre to visit Mrs Craven. She found her sitting at the kitchen table drinking tea, still dressed in her housecoat.

'Good of you to come, Fiona. I'm sorry our Cathy has caused so much trouble for everyone, but we'll sort her out. Her father's getting special leave. He'll be home by this evening, and the hospital telephoned to tell me that I can go and fetch Cathy at midday.'

'That's good news. I doubt if she's suffered any ill effects from the experiment, and now that she realises it can bring on an asthmatic attack she'll probably never get involved again.'

'It's those friends,' Mrs Craven sobbed. She looked heavy-eyed with dark circles made more prominent by pale cheeks. It looked as if she had suffered a sleepless night. 'Why, Fiona? Haven't we given her a good home? Treated her fairly as we thought was best for her? How could she bring this shame on us? Whatever do those kids get out of sniffing glue? It's revolting.'

'Usually it's a craze, Mrs Craven. It's sometimes like an epidemic which goes through schools. They all have to try it, then they start jobs and some move on and for the moment the craze dies down.'

'But why, Fiona?'

'Excitement. It's something they can sneak away and do, knowing they shouldn't be doing it. It's not a punishable offence until they get so that they don't know what they're doing, then of course they're in trouble if they commit a crime.'

'How does it actually affect them? I'm afraid I'm a bit ignorant.'

'A few deep breaths of solvent sniffing can produce a feeling of euphoria. It may last a few minutes or even half an hour. If they continue to inhale then it can give them a high and become dangerous. The sniffer may have hallucinations, and eventually can lose consciousness. They're usually horribly sick—you'd think that was enough to put them off. It's debatable whether anyone would become physically dependent on solvent sniffing, but psychologically it is possible. Research shows that when sniffing continues after teenage it is frequently a call for help. As so often with drug-taking there's usually a more deep seated reason for escape than merely being curious.'

'Goodness knows what her father will say. He'll hit the roof.'

'That's understandable, but it won't solve anything. She needs something to do. Would you like me to have a word at the Job Centre?'

Mrs Craven sighed. 'If they can't find work for most of last year's school leavers what hope is there for Cathy? Up till now she's refused to take any further courses at college, but we'll have to see what her father says.'

Fiona was in two minds whether or not to go into Gorton to see Cathy as she was due to be discharged shortly, but she decided she should keep her word and when she reached the ward Cathy was nowhere to be found.

'We've given her something to do,' Sister Gisborne said. 'There's a young girl here with asthma. She's had it mildly since quite young, but now in her early teens the attacks have become more frequent, and are more severe. Lisa gets terrified so we thought Cathy could talk to her and perhaps explain how she copes.'

'That's a good idea. They can console one another. I promised I'd come so I'll just say hullo.'

'I'll go and fetch her. Bet you've only come because you can't keep away from the hospital.'

Fiona laughed. 'Does have a certain attraction, I must say. You never get hospital life out of your blood, do you?'

'I don't know, I wouldn't even try, but, Fiona, you're a health visitor. Shouldn't a social worker be dealing with Cathy's case?'

'Dave's got his hands full as it is, and as I know the family, and knew Cathy from school, I'm following it up. Addiction of all kinds is getting more common. We ought to get more help groups going, especially out in the suburbs. Everyone thinks it can't happen in their district, then the next thing they know it's right on their doorstep.'

'At least television is trying to emphasise the dangers. I suppose we must be thankful for the few who are too frightened to experiment. I feel certain Cathy won't ever try it again.' Sister Gisborne went off, returning with her arm around Cathy's shoulders.

'Hullo, Cathy. How d'you feel today?' Fiona said.

Sister Gisborne guided Cathy into a nearby empty room, and Fiona followed.

'I'm fine, Fiona.' The young girl's eyes filled with tears and her lip trembled. 'I'm sorry I did it—went off with the others—but I'm glad it was you who found me. I just didn't know where to go.'

'What was the matter with going home?'

'I guessed that Mum would have sent for Dad.' She entwined her fingers and clasped them tightly until they turned to porcelain white.

'It would have been wiser to think of that first, Cathy. You're not afraid of him, are you?'

Cathy buried her face in her hands. 'I . . . I'm so ashamed. I always promised them I'd never let anyone talk me into trying drugs and things. I never realised that just sniffing a piece of rag would bring on my asthma. I . . . I don't think the others knew what was happening. They thought I was pretending—oh—it was *awful*, Fiona.' She paused while she sobbed and then it was as if everything had to come tumbling out. 'I love my Dad, I hated leaving London, all my friends were there. I've never really had a special friend here. Dad *is* strict —well, whenever he comes home Mum delights in telling him what a nuisance I am. She hates having me round the house all day, but it isn't my fault I can't get a job.'

'I think your parents are just going to be relieved that you're all right, Cathy, and hope that one experiment has been enough to make sure you say "no", and a very firm *no* from now on. It won't be easy, we all hate being different from our friends, but at least you've got an important reason for saying no. Now that your friends realise that you suffer from asthma, and have seen how easily an attack can be brought on by inhaling solvents, maybe they'll think twice before indulging in the habit again. Maybe your experience will influence them for the better. Cathy, never be afraid to ring me up if you get into bother, or Patsy who isn't all that much older than you. We're going to see if we can't start some sort of help group in our area. We care about our young people, and we hate to see them destroying themselves.'

'I wish Mum was as easy to talk to as you, Fiona.'

'I'm sure she is, Cathy, if only you'd give her the chance. Try treating her like your best friend, then she'll suddenly see you as an adult instead of a stubborn little girl. Of course your parents will never stop worrying about you, mine still worry about me.'

Cathy looked up at Fiona in disbelief and Fiona laughed. 'Yes, Cathy, I've got two lovely parents, but they live up North since my father retired. When things get on top of me I feel I just want to pack my bags and run home to them.' Fiona noticed the hint of a smile soften Cathy's expression.

'But you're a big girl now, aren't you Cathy, so you've got to show your parents that you can handle any situation.'

Fiona knew by the sudden sparkle in Cathy's eyes that someone had come into the room. She turned in response to the firm hand on her shoulder and found herself looking straight up into Stephen's face.

'Hullo, Cathy,' he said with a broad, friendly smile. 'How is it this morning?'

'I'm all right, thanks,' she replied meekly. 'Mum's coming in to fetch me at midday. There's some kind of lady doctor they want us both to see before I leave —about my asthma, I think.'

'I'm glad you're okay,' Fiona said gently, escaping Stephen's hand and standing up to leave. 'I'll be in to see you and your parents tomorrow.'

'I'll need you,' Cathy whispered in a husky voice, and Fiona could see how frightened she really was.

Was Mr Craven a bit over-powering? Fiona wondered. She couldn't interfere, but she would make a visit to the Craven household very shortly. As Stephen stood aside to let her pass she was acutely aware of her body's reaction to his nearness. To be close to James was warm and comforting, a little like the feeling of security she experienced when in the company of her parents, but this rising passion which flowed through every blood vessel and set her nerve ends dancing with elation was something she'd forgotten she was capable of. She had thought that such feelings had been crushed along with her pelvis, damaged beyond repair, so it came as a pleasant surprise to find that her body still had a will of its own.

'Heavy schedule?' Stephen asked.

'Yes, it's clinic day and I've a few calls to make before then,' she said excusing herself as she walked uncertainly away.

As she hurried across the busy car-park she managed to steady her heartbeats. She was glad that Stephen was visiting Cathy because by the look of admiration in the younger girl's eyes she too was affected by his good looks and pleasing manner. If Stephen didn't care one way or another about a new primary school Fiona felt sure he would support her in forming a help group for drug addicts.

On her round she passed Sue Pines' road and stopped off to enquire how she was coping, but there was no one at home, so she visited an elderly gentleman recently widowed, and two young mothers just home from the maternity wing of Gorton hospital, and then she returned to the health centre for an early lunch. Patsy wasn't in yet, but a peep inside Lizzie's room showed Fiona that she had been back for elevenses and had prepared the room for the afternoon clinic. She was a good, keen worker, and Fiona experienced a motherly affection for her young assistant.

After a brief visit to the almost empty canteen for coffee and a cheese roll, Fiona returned to her office. Everything prepared for the afternoon clinic, she took out her notebook and began a list of things she needed to bring up at tomorrow's practice meeting. Cathy's name headed the list, after which she wrote: Group therapy. Help group, and then followed a reminder of the people who might be willing to help. The vicar, school teachers, as well as doctors, nurses, and social workers. There were some retired professional people who might be glad to help too, but were they in the wrong age-group? she wondered, tapping her teeth with the end of her pen. She was a little sceptical about the reaction she would get. Everyone seemed to try to avoid talking about the drug problem for fear it would attract attention and encourage youngsters to experiment, but time and study was proving this to be an incorrect supposition. She must begin her campaign of nipping it in the bud by giving lectures at all the local schools. Not so much a lecture she decided as a nice homely chat, and perhaps Cathy would agree to accompany her and tell her own story. There were video films she could get, pretty horrific she remembered from her recent course, but perhaps this was the right time to shock parents and youngsters alike.

When Fiona went along to Lizzie's room just before two o'clock she found a pram already in the porch and Sue Pines was drinking tea and chatting to Katie.

'My goodness, Sue, you're an early bird.'

Sue looked bright and cheerful, still pale, but her eyes held a look of confidence.

'I'm meeting Anita Boughton and we're going into Gorton to do some shopping.'

'That's good. Yes, Lucy and Daniel are almost the same age. Are you going on the bus?'

'Yes, but we're leaving the babes with Mrs Craven and Cathy. Mrs Craven thought it might help ease the tension with all that's happened.'

'It'll take Cathy's mind off having to face her father. You're looking better, Sue. I called in this morning. How is Daniel?'

'I still worry,' she said solemnly, her expression changing to one of concern, 'but Dr O'Neal checked him over and says he's fine; she noticed how pale I was and took a blood test then she visited me a couple of days later with some iron pills.' Sue smiled. 'I can't tell you how much better I feel already, Fiona. You were right, I was run down, which made everything such an effort, and I got things out of proportion.'

'Better to be over concerned than not concerned enough, but I'm glad to see you so much brighter. Come on, young Danny-boy, let's get you weighed.'

While Fiona checked Danny and chatted to Sue she noticed that Patsy arrived at the same time as Anita Boughton with Lucy. She attended to them next so that the two young mums could go off for a few hours' freedom.

It was a warm, sunny afternoon, and after the first rush only a straggle of mothers and babies attended the clinic, and they were able to pack up soon after four o'clock.

As Fiona sat at her desk not really paying too much attention to Patsy's chatter she wondered what was happening at the Craven household. She was very curious about the much feared Mr Craven who she hoped to meet the following day.

It seemed as if James must have been watching for Patsy's departure for only seconds after the sound of her heels faded down the passage, the door opened again and James walked in.

Fiona was closing her briefcase, and James came to stand at the front of her desk.

'Ready to go?' he asked.

'Mm—not a large clinic today. Perry got off lightly.'

'So he reported. Are we set for our usual dinner date?'

Fiona glanced across at him, suspicious of the tone of indifference in his voice.

'Not if you want to do something else, James.'

'Why should I?' His handsome face wrinkled with sudden amusement. 'Why should this Tuesday be different from any other?'

'I just thought you sounded—tired.' The word tripped easily off her tongue, when she really meant that she suspected he was tiring of her, but looking at him closely she noticed that his eyes had warmed to her. He was a man who liked women, enjoyed their femininity, was fascinated by their many facets and intrigued by their sexuality.

Something inside her stirred. Why had she doubted his feelings for her? Was it because she doubted her own feelings for him? Yet, as they stood facing one another, the only barrier three feet of desk, Fiona experienced the comfortable ease magnetise them together, and she responded to his admiration of her with trusting devotion. His coolness was all in her mind. James hadn't changed at all, he was still the kind, understanding man she had grown to love. Kind, understanding. Words that echoed in her brain through Stephen's voice. A voice that reminded her of disloyalty, but to which of them?

She closed her case with decisive clicks, avoiding James' eyes.

'I'm always tired,' he said with a grin, 'but never too tired to dine with you. Shall we go out or—'

'I haven't prepared anything, but I can soon rustle up something,' Fiona said.

James stretched. 'It looks like being a nice evening. Can you manage something quick and easy so that we can go for a nice long walk with Cass, maybe stop off at a pub for a drink?'

Fiona felt herself sag. She could have done with an early night, but maybe the weather was too good to waste.

'Mm—okay,' she said, her spirits lifting. 'How about sausage and mash?'

James pulled a face, then he made a grab for her and held her fast while his lips met hers with sweet sincerity. So sweet, in fact, that Fiona made no attempt to pull away until a surreptitious cough made her glance towards the doorway where Stephen was standing, taking in the intimate scene with a brooding look of distaste in his dark eyes, and a crooked smile of mockery round his mouth.

CHAPTER NINE

'DON'T mind me,' he said sarcastically. 'I thought you'd like to know that Cathy Craven is home, Fiona.'

Fiona felt a tide of heat rush over her, and became more embarrassed when James kept his hand firmly round her neck refusing to let go.

'Yes, I did know.' There was a distinct tone of petulance in her voice. He knew she knew, hadn't she been there at the hospital at the same time as he?

'And Mr Craven too,' he went on pointedly. 'I realised you wouldn't be able to visit today because you had clinic duty, so as I had an emergency call in that direction I took the opportunity of popping in.'

'I wasn't sure when he was expected so I thought I'd wait until tomorrow. Are things a bit strained?'

Stephen came farther into the room as Fiona picked up her case and moved away from the desk.

'Surprisingly, no. It's true Mr Craven had only been home an hour or so, but Cathy seemed quite relaxed, though I suspect Mrs Craven was being a bit over-jolly.'

'I'll visit tomorrow anyway,' Fiona said.

'I met Mr Craven when they first moved here from London,' James said thoughtfully. 'It's a long while ago now—oh, and I believe he had a bad virus one Christmas when he was home on leave.' James pushed his hands deep into his pockets and swayed on one foot surveying Stephen. 'He's the type of man you don't forget. Physically insignificant, but mentally very much the boss. I fancy something's not quite as it should be, though I have no grounds for saying such a thing.'

Stephen took a deep breath. 'You could be right, James. I sensed a slight tension in Mrs Craven. Guess that's not our affair though. It's Cathy we have to watch.'

James drew level with Fiona as she edged round her desk. He placed an arm protectively round her shoulders. 'I'm sure Fiona has that high on the agenda for the practice meeting tomorrow.'

Stephen took the hint and backed out of the open doorway. 'You two off somewhere nice this evening?'

James laughed. 'Sausage and mash, I believe. A run in the park or forest, and a nightcap at our favourite pub.'

'Don't tell anyone, James, it sounds pathetic,' Fiona protested with amusement.

'Lucky you to have each other to share an evening. You probably won't even notice that it is sausage and mash.'

Fiona met his piercing stare with sympathy in her eyes. She guessed he was sending them up in a light-hearted way, perhaps even being sarcastic about their relationship, but in two short sentences he had dropped his guard, making her realise how much he missed his wife, and how devoted he was to her memory. Lucky Stephen, she thought with a touch of envy, he had found true love even if it had been snatched from him.

He stood aside to let Fiona pass and then followed James down the stairs.

'While you enjoy your sausage and mash spare a thought for the workers,' he said. 'I'm on call this evening, so I miss out on bath time at home, my most favourite time of day.'

Fiona felt her mouth go dry, but she managed a curt

'Cheerio' as she crossed the reception hall to the swing doors. Little did he know how her heart ached with longing whenever she held a baby in her arms. Therapeutic though it may be, her work of caring for mums, babies and toddlers also made her inability to bear children a fact which she could never ignore. Stephen had lost his wife, and Fiona felt a genuine sorrow for him, but he had a future with his children, and in a way love for his wife would continue through them while Fiona had nothing. She remained silent as she and James walked side by side across the car-park. It was almost as if James knew of her heartache which had faded with time, but was now very much revived.

'I'll just pop home first, darling,' he said, 'to see if there's any post or messages, as I've been here all day. I'll have a wash and brush up and see you in an hour.' He stood close to Fiona as she unlocked her car door, and kissed her cheek swiftly, adding a pat on her bottom which was uncharacteristic of James.

She managed a hesitant smile. 'Give me time to do my worst with the sausages and mash,' she quipped, and James left her to go to his own car.

Fiona drove away without a backward glance. Dear James, she was so fond of him, but did he understand fully how much she needed a man's love? She knew that Stephen was right inasmuch as kindness and understanding was insufficient to make a marriage complete, even at their age. James at forty-four was still a virile man, and she at thirty-two should have plenty of sexual desire to stimulate a relationship, but now passionate thoughts of intimacy between herself and James had been replaced by old exciting memories of the way things had been before the accident.

*   *   *

Cass greeted her enthusiastically and Fiona let her out into the garden while she showered and changed into a green floral cotton dress, then with a surreptitious smile she defrosted the sausages and peeled potatoes. While they were boiling she grilled the sausages, adding a rasher of bacon, at the last moment deciding to scramble some eggs as well.

James arrived looking fresh and cool in some light hopsack trousers and a dark brown open-necked shirt. As they sat down he laughed at the substantial meal set before him.

'Sausage and mash fully dressed up, I see. It looks and smells good, darling.'

He was always appreciative of her allowing him to share her meals. He had a good housekeeper who worked for him four mornings a week, and she often left everything ready for cooking, but Fiona was glad of his company. Well—she had been up until recently, but the orderliness of the past few years was changing. The father figure of Dr Locke was no longer in evidence, and the relationship between herself and James was different. Part father-figure, part—lover? No, they weren't lovers in the true sense. They might have been growing towards intimacy, but even such anticipation had dimmed over the past week or two.

'The holiday camp site looked busy as I drove through,' James said.

'The nice weather always brings a few people in, but once the school holidays start it'll be full up I expect. Rain or shine, every rented caravan gets taken and the tents go up. It's nice to be in a peaceful environment, but it's fun to be surrounded by holidaymakers and Mr and Mrs Hollis serve them well. They work long hours, and it's tiring work even if the season is fairly short.'

'I'm glad they have their mobile home next to yours. I don't like you being so isolated in the winter and they're often away as soon as the season ends. Still, I hope it won't be too long before you make up your mind to come and share my flat.'

'I can't imagine living anywhere but here, James.' She spoke sincerely, not aiming to hurt him, but by the dark frown which puckered his brow she knew she had.

'Well you don't expect me to move in here with you, surely?'

Fiona turned it into a joke. 'Why not? You seem to enjoy coming here.'

'That's true—yes, I suppose it would make an ideal weekend retreat, but I must admit I'd visualised us both selling up and buying a nice house near the river perhaps.'

'That's a long way off, James,' Fiona said simply. She expected some persuasion to follow but he appeared to accept this without question and a few moments later changed the subject.

After they had eaten he helped her with the dishes, and then they set off in James' car. Cassie enjoyed the long stroll by the river and was glad to rest under an outside table at Fiona and James' favourite pub called the Carp and Cod, which was renowned for its variety of fish dishes both at the bar and in the restaurant. But all they needed was a reviving drink sipped leisurely while they watched a family of swans nesting on the far river bank, and an occasional small boat passing by.

Back at Fiona's home they watched the late news while enjoying a cup of tea, and then James stood up to go. Fiona was totally unprepared for the savage embrace when James crushed her to him. His mouth was hard on hers at first then gently became more supple, and she found herself kissing him back with fervour, but when his hands began to explore and caress, she felt herself stiffen. She tried to check the protest that was foremost in her mind, but it was unnecessary as James drew back, gazed at her with burning desire reflected in his eyes, and with a laugh said, 'Forgive me, darling, I got carried away. You're quite the enchantress you know, sausage and mash to boot.'

They laughed together, but not as easily as on previous occasions for Fiona knew that such demonstrative passion was a sham. Before Stephen returned she had forced herself to try to love again, but had never quite succeeded. She felt so guilty at hurting the man for whom she felt sincere respect, and was genuinely fond of. With another light kiss James said good night and left. Fiona sat curled up on the settee and tried to sort out her muddled thoughts. Not muddled about her own emotions for she knew now that she could never marry James, though how she was going to tell him she couldn't imagine. She was confused about him. He'd previously been first a good friend and colleague, and only gradually had affection played any part. Even then it was a quiet reserved kind of emotion that occasionally led to love-making in a mild, contented way, but tonight he had indicated a strength of sexual prowess she hadn't bargained for. Was he trying to force her to make a final decision? He knew nothing of her past relationship with Stephen, or was he observant enough to have noticed some hidden liaison?

It was well past one a.m. when Fiona slipped beneath her light summer duvet. Sleep evaded her cruelly, and no sooner had her enigmatic doubts faded than her alarm bell screamed throughout her mobile home with the urgency of a fire-bell. She got herself up feeling dreadful, and even after a quick jog round the site, picking up her paper from Mr Hollis on her return, she felt no better. It was going to be a hell of a day, she thought dismally. The Cravens to visit, the local school if there was time, and the dreaded practice meeting. As she sipped coffee and bit on some unpalatable toast she decided that the school visit might be better postponed to the following day after she had put certain proposals forward at today's meeting. There was only one way to forget her personal problems and that was to work non-stop, and if her ideas were accepted it would mean precious little time for a private life anyway.

During the first hour in her office she briefed Patsy on her proposed agenda, and then while Patsy started her round of visits to the elderly, and one or two young mums recently home with new babies, Fiona drove to the Cravens' house.

There was only one word to describe the atmosphere as Mrs Craven invited Fiona in, and that was subdued. Had there been a big row which left everyone drained, or was this the prelude to an eruption?

'And who might this young lady be?' The ordinary looking man emerging from behind a morning newspaper spoke in a curious tone laced with contempt. Fiona sussed him out at once as being a masterful man who disliked outside interference. James, she guessed, had summed Mr Craven up accurately.

'Miss Meredith, our local health visitor at the Centre,' Mrs Craven introduced.

'Fiona, please. How do you do, Mr Craven.' She held out her hand politely, and the man stood up with leisurely indifference. He was about the same height as Fiona and they surveyed one another coolly. 'How's Cathy this morning?' she asked.

'Perfectly fit, young lady. All this nonsense is a storm in a teacup.' He took her hand briefly but strongly.

'One isolated case may seem so to you, Mr Craven,' Fiona said, standing her ground, 'but statistics prove otherwise. Glue-sniffing is an extremely dangerous practice.'

'Then the law should stop it,' he snapped.

'Legislation takes time to be put into practice, but just because it's against the law for solvents to be sold to anyone under the age of eighteen now doesn't mean that if they've a mind to they'll get hold of glue one way or another. In many instances once youngsters have tried it out and become violently ill they don't do it again, but in today's sad world when they go on abusing themselves by sniffing solvents or taking drugs it's invariably a cry for help. Broken homes being the most common cause.'

Mr Craven crumpled his paper against his chest.

'Now look here, young lady, just because I happen to live in London——'

'I'm stating facts, Mr Craven. It's not my job to moralise or cast judgment. I just want to help Cathy.'

Fiona sensed that Cathy had come into the room. The girl stood behind her and smiled hesitantly as Fiona turned to her.

'No more breathing problems, Cathy?' Fiona asked.

'I bought this house here in a rural area hoping it would effect a cure,' Mr Craven cut in acidly.

'She has been better,' Mrs Craven intervened softly.

'But I didn't want to leave London,' Cathy put in quickly. She glanced awkwardly from her father to her mother. 'All my friends are there. I want to work in London.'

It was Mr and Mrs Craven's turn to look at each other awkwardly. There was something between them. Fiona couldn't put her finger on it but she sensed a barrier of sorts.

'Your parents are right in believing that country air should suit you better than the city, Cathy,' Fiona said. 'As far as your asthma is concerned.'

Mr Craven sat down and endeavoured, without much success, to fold the newspaper tidily. 'Sit down all of you,' he commanded, then to his wife, 'Put the kettle on.'

'I'm hoping to start a self-help group, Cathy,' Fiona said. 'Would you come with me and tell others about your experiences?'

'Indeed she will *not*!'

'Mr Craven, we have to try to warn our youngsters against the dangers. It's only natural that they don't like to be different from their friends. I expect you did things when you were a boy rather than be called "chicken"?'

'Nothing as dreadful as kids do today,' he mumbled.

'Your first cigarette, your first drink, even scrumping apples was considered dreadful then.'

'Yes, I got a belting for all three and a few more misdemeanours besides.' He sighed. 'Now those things seem mild by comparison. I don't understand the kids of today. We never had any trouble with Anita.'

'I realise how difficult it is for you working away from home and with the added worry of unemployment for Cathy. It isn't her fault, but there should be something she can do to fill her time.'

'Can I come back to London with you, Dad?' Cathy's plea was in earnest. 'I can look after you and the flat, and perhaps find work.'

'Sounds to me as if we need to discuss the situation in more detail,' her father acknowledged. 'It's very good of you to call, Miss—er—Fiona. I'm home for a break. If we need you we'll call you.'

It was a neat dismissal, but Fiona felt that perhaps it had only been her presence there that had given Cathy the courage to tell her parents that she would prefer to live in London.

During the afternoon practice meeting when Fiona reported her visit to the Cravens, James replied with: 'Surely the temptations will be worse for Cathy in London?'

'On the face of it one would think so, but she grew up there. It's her home ground, she knows the city, and she still has friends there. It obviously threw her parents when she said she wanted to go to live with her father.'

'Mother and daughter relationship not too good by the sound of things,' Perry said.

'By outward appearances they seem all right, but I did sense something of an atmosphere. My main concern is Cathy, which leads me to the next point on my agenda and that is setting up a self-help group for the youngsters, or a help group anyway.'

'What is this, the Fiona Meredith show?' Perry quipped.

'I'm sorry to hog the meeting——' she began.

'First petitions, now help groups,' he chided.

'I think Fiona is right,' Stephen said. 'I've been reading up about the dependency of glue-sniffing which mustn't be confused with drug addiction. The youngsters can start the practice for fun from the age of ten. It can lead to habitual sniffing, and deaths have occurred. I suspect most parents don't know how to handle the situation, and up to now GPs have turned a blind eye. That's not good enough, we must surely take a keen interest, get involved with the youngsters and act before they're brought to us for medical treatment. I've got children of my own—prevention is better than cure.'

'I agree,' Brian Sandford said. 'From what I've read about it the type of school or background they come from will make no difference. How do you propose to organise such a group, Fiona?'

'The village hall could be used, or the new church hall, and—well—' Fiona hunched her shoulders and gripped her pen, 'volunteer helpers—*please*?'

There was a stony silence while Dave, the social worker, eyed Fiona knowingly, then his gaze flitted round the oblong table from James to Stephen, and on to Brian and Perry. Fiona wished that Laura was present as she felt the odd one out being the only woman.

'It is another claim on our time, Fiona,' James began.

'But we can't claim to be overworked,' Stephen said forcefully. 'Gone are the days when two doctors took turns for morning and evening surgeries six days a week and sometimes an emergency session on Sundays, not to mention being on call for twenty-four hours a day. There are five of us so we're talking about once a month, I suppose, aren't we, Fiona?'

'It depends how it goes. Certainly a regular weekly group to begin with, and I'm prepared to go it alone for the first couple of months. After all, I know so many of our youngsters from school.'

'Definitely *not*.' Stephen's commanding voice surprised everyone. 'You may start a group for solvent sniffers, but who's to say other drug addicts or alcoholics won't turn up for help? It wouldn't be right for a woman to be on duty alone.'

'Fiona knows that I'm one hundred per cent behind her,' Dave said. 'As social worker this is my province.'

'But you're already heavily committed,' Fiona said with gratitude.

'If you can do it then so will I. My job brings me into contact with the youngsters most likely to be affected.'

James leaned back in his chair asserting his authority. 'I feel this is a worthwhile enterprise but it should be shared by all in the community. The vicar and other churchmen, teachers, retired doctors perhaps, and nurses. There are many resources we can tap and hopefully once it gets known others will come forward, but I agree with Stephen, it's not a job Fiona should tackle alone.'

'We can get a speaker down from London who is very knowledgeable about the subject,' she suggested. 'He'll bring a film which, horrific though it may be, should be shown to parents, then we might get the back-up we need.'

James smiled affectionately at Fiona. 'You've been doing your homework.'

'Not difficult, James, as I get a great deal of literature from headquarters on how to deal with the problem. I didn't think we had much of a problem here but Cathy has made me all too aware of it. We mustn't be complacent just because we're in a rural area. Gorton is a growing town and it's becoming easier for the youngsters to get into Gorton to sample the night-life. One disco a week at the church hall here isn't sufficient to keep our kids near home, but now that some of them are going into Gorton it means the Gorton youngsters are visiting us. I feel it's our duty to show them that help is available —easier here perhaps than in the town.'

Fiona felt agreeably pleased that her suggestion had been listened to, and seemingly pricked a few consciences. Stephen may have refused to get involved with the petition for a new primary school, but he was certainly backing her where this project was concerned, and as the meeting progressed and Fiona reported that the Abilenes living at the small-holding were refusing any kind of help during Mrs Abilene's pregnancy, it was Stephen who offered his services.

'I'll make a nuisance of myself and try to talk them round,' he said. 'It isn't as if they live a few doors away from a hospital, nor do you operate the system here of having continuous care by a midwife and GP and the pregnant woman only goes into hospital for a six-hour stay for the actual confinement. They live in an isolated area and as it's a first baby she should have all the available tests. Whose list is she actually on?'

'Laura's,' James divulged. 'When Fiona told me about this young couple I looked up the records. Mrs Abilene is registered, not the husband. I mentioned it to Laura, but she—um—has—er—personal problems to deal with at present, so I've given her a few days off. She did try to persuade Mrs Abilene to sign a pregnancy form, but she said she'd have to ask her husband first so Laura decided it might be as well not to rush things. That's why it was passed on to you, Fiona.'

'I wish Laura had discussed the case with me before I went up there on a wild goose chase,' Fiona said.

'I'll apologise for her, my dear,' James said, emulating Dr Locke's fatherly manner, 'but as I said she has a lot on her plate at present.'

'I'll see what I can do,' Stephen reiterated. 'Home deliveries are quite the thing in some areas of Australia, but then we had the Flying Doctor, and instant contact by radio. I don't mind taking responsibility for a home delivery with Meggie, but only provided that Mrs Abilene has been given the go ahead by the hospital.

There must be no suspicion of any abnormality.'

'All help was firmly refused,' Fiona said.

'We'll just have to keep trying,' Stephen answered with a smile.

Fiona decided she had better keep quiet for the remainder of the meeting, so at four o'clock when Katie rattled up to the door with the tea-trolley Fiona got up and brought it inside, pouring out and passing the tea round.

In her eagerness to get her help groups going she allowed her mind to streak ahead in that direction thinking that perhaps dear Dr Locke would recover sufficiently to be involved, and then she realised what James was saying. The meeting was being brought to a close, and James in his own charming manner was welcoming Stephen to the practice on a permanent basis, and suggesting that a celebratory dinner would be a nice idea.

'Spouses included, and for those without, a guest. How about it, Stephen?'

'Sounds a splendid idea, count me in—yes, I can bring a guest—and I'll provide the champagne,' Stephen said eagerly.

CHAPTER TEN

I<small>T</small> wasn't what Stephen had said, but the implications behind it. Fiona's mind leapt ahead in enormous strides. A guest already lined up to accompany him to the dinner? Fiona's spirits drooped to an all time low. She had accepted the fact that he was back, that he was widowed, but she'd never imagined him with a lady-friend already.

The door opened and Meggie burst in.

'Sorry I couldn't make it—one of Mrs Hartnell's neighbours collared me as they hadn't seen her around since yesterday.'

'I was there yesterday,' Fiona said. 'She's all right, isn't she?'

'She is now. We had to bang on the doors and windows to get her to open up. She managed to get to the door eventually, but she looked as if she'd been beaten up. I contacted one of her daughters, and the local policeman who lives round the corner, but there's no sign of a break-in. She doesn't remember what happened after you left, Fiona. In fact she thought you ought to still be there.'

'Where is she now?'

'In hospital. A geriatric ward, just until she gets sorted out in her mind. Her bruises and wounds are only superficial, but naturally she's in shock and at times seems rather confused, poor dear. Cups and saucers were still on the table, but there was a trail of blood from her airing cupboard on the landing. It's a big one, she

134

keeps steps and things in it so we think she must have been trying to reach something and fell.'

'Poor Mrs Hartnell.'

'She oughtn't to be there on her own, and she should let one of her girls have a key.'

'You can't force her to give up her independence in one fell swoop, Meggie,' Fiona insisted. 'She'll take some persuading, and we'll have to do it bit by bit.'

'She's safe enough for a day or two. What have I missed?—anything important?' Meggie was always in a rush.

James told her about the proposed dinner party and diaries were consulted as to a suitable date.

'The Cod and Carp have a nice little room for private functions,' James said. 'Let's see, there's nine of us plus the girls outside, and Katie, of course, so with guests we should be about twenty.'

Everyone voiced their approval, and the coming Friday evening was decided upon, but it was all too sudden for Fiona. She was finding it extremely difficult working with both James and Stephen. Her emotions refused to stay under control and this led to a feeling of disloyalty to James—to have to be in their company at a social function and as James' companion made her expectancy of the event nothing but embarrassment.

Laura didn't return to duty that week so Fiona was surprised when James announced that they would be picking Laura up en route to the Cod and Carp.

'She's not bringing her husband then?' Fiona said with surprise.

'He's away a great deal, and I thought it would be a nice gesture to make sure she had a lift there and back. You girls can enjoy Stephen's champagne without having to worry about driving home.'

'I'm not that keen on champagne. I'm sure I shall be in a fit state to drive, so for a change you can indulge if you want to.'

'I can't imagine any of us over-indulging,' James retorted.

Fiona thought he seemed a little on edge, but once they had picked Laura up at her luxury flat and were greeting the others at the bar of the Cod and Carp he seemed to relax, while Fiona grew more tense.

The pub was quite crowded, being a Friday evening, so James ordered drinks for everyone and a waiter carried them out to a far corner of the garden overlooking the river. It was soon evident that Laura wanted to discuss some personal problem with James. Fiona wasn't that curious, but she did wonder what all the secrecy was about, and where was Laura's husband this evening? He was usually at home weekends, Fiona knew, even though she had never met him. She discreetly moved away from the others when she saw Stephen parking his car. She watched with idle curiosity as he hurried round to the passenger's side and a tall, elegantly slim, ravishing blonde girl uncurled her shapely legs to get out of the car. They were laughing together as he locked up, and Fiona couldn't bear to look. Pain gnawed at her inside as if she was being eaten alive. Not jealousy, she pleaded with her emotions, not now after all these years, and knowing that he had been married, happily, and was now the father of three children. Surely it was too late, and she too mature for jealousy to engulf her. But it was evident, and no matter how she fought against it the pain increased. She walked to the river bank, watching the swans, anything to defer the introduction, but James came after her.

'Come on, darling, our table is ready, we can go in.'

He put his arm round her waist, and Fiona knew that he was looking at her with a puzzled frown. 'If I haven't said so already, you look very lovely tonight. What shade of blue do you call it?'

'Mm,' she tried to laugh off his flattery. 'Sort of midnight blue, I think, it's too bright for a true royal.'

'It's a perfect shade for you, seems to make your eyes look like velvet, and the style is most elegant.'

At any other time she would have found his compliments pleasing, but the feel of his fingers penetrating the jersey silk of her dress irritated her beyond endurance, and yet endure she must, for she was his companion for the evening. The only compensation she had was the fact that she knew her dress was stunning. It should be, she reflected, a picture of the price tag in her mind's eye, but she had loved it the moment Madame Simone had put it on the model in the window of the small exclusive boutique on the Gorton Road. Fiona had needed to visit Simone's ageing father after a major operation, and when Simone had in a flourish of French assured Fiona that she had made the dress with her in mind, offering a substantial discount, Fiona had succumbed to the temptation. A perfect engagement dress, or perhaps a 'going away' dress she had thought at the time, and tonight on a sudden impulse she had weakened and decided to wear it on what she had thought in her subconscious might be a special occasion. She didn't feel over-dressed for the style was a simple figure-flattering one with long slim sleeves buttoned at the wrist, and the bodice was gathered into a small yoke at the shoulders forming a low vee-neck. Fiona had decided on white button ear-rings and a white bead choker. High-heeled, narrow-strapped sandals, and her tights and clutch bag all matched her dress exactly. Too blue she had thought when she viewed her reflection in the mirror, but now it matched her mood.

The others were manoeuvering their way into the restaurant but Stephen was waiting by the door. His dark eyes were warm yet bright with anticipation as he appraised Fiona's appearance.

'Hullo, Fiona,' he greeted, 'you look quite the regal hostess tonight.'

Fiona frowned with disapproval. 'Not regal, please,' she said. 'Makes me sound at least fifty, and I'm not the hostess.'

'Of course you are, as James' companion. I'd like you to meet Anna Krohne.'

Out of politeness Fiona was obliged to smile at the girl by Stephen's side as they shook hands. She was a few inches taller than Fiona, almost the same height as Stephen and they instantly registered as being ideally suited.

'How do you do,' Fiona said, as she was forced to meet the other girl's gaze from pale blue, laughing eyes with a hint of devillish mischief in them. Anna's skin was porcelain white, her sensuously full lips accentuated by the crimson lipstick she wore which matched her red linen suit. She's young, Fiona thought, very early twenties—was she perhaps a replica of his late wife?

'Anna originates from Sweden,' Stephen explained briefly.

Fiona smiled, and Anna threw back her long blonde hair as she said, 'I'm very happy to be here in England, the climate is very good. I wish to study English.'

'But your English sounds perfect to me,' Fiona said.

'There is room for much improvement, I think,' Anna said laughingly, and then James pushed Fiona on into the smallish, unfamiliar room. It had only recently been

opened and was decorated in keeping with the Olde
Worlde inn image with wooden wall panels, red velvet
curtains, dark red and grey patterned carpet, and
Jacobean-style furniture. Glass cases of stuffed cod
and carp were the only link with the name of the inn,
yet the atmosphere of river fishing, fishermen and
boats spilled over from the main bar.

A large oval table was set for twenty people and the
centre attraction, instead of the usual floral decoration,
was of an elegant tall ship in full illuminated sail. It was
an instant object of admiration as was each individual
place setting signified by small silver yachts lit up by
slow-burning candles hidden inside.

James organised the seating arrangements. In fact it
became obvious that he had visited the Cod and Carp
earlier in the day to arrange the name cards. His place
was in the centre of one of the long sides of the table with
Laura at his right hand side and Fiona on the left. Anna
was placed immediately opposite James and Stephen
was directly across the table from Fiona. She hardly
noticed where everyone else sat, but she was grateful to
have Brian and his wife, Alison, next to her, and soon
her confusion was drowned by the babble of voices.

The meal was a large one, celery soup to start with,
followed by smoked salmon as befitted a riverside inn.
There was a variety of main courses and Fiona chose
roast pork and apple sauce with an assortment of fresh
vegetables. By the time the sweet trolley came round
Fiona had little room for anything else, but she allowed
herself to be persuaded to a small piece of lemon and
walnut gâteau, and the consumption of good white wine
quickly dispelled her blue mood. Finally, before coffee
and liqueurs were served, the champagne glasses were
filled to capacity and James proposed the toast to a long

and harmonious partnership with Stephen as second senior doctor. A telegram of good wishes was read out from Dr Locke and his wife, and in response Stephen made a suitable reply and toasted Dr Locke's recovery to good health. Everyone was in convivial mood until Brian's wife raised her glass to James and Fiona.

'Come on you two,' she said light-heartedly, 'can't we make this a double celebration? It's time you put a ring on Fiona's finger, James and stopped all the rumours and speculations.'

James drew Fiona towards him, awkwardly as there was considerable space between each seat. 'She has only to name the day,' he said in a low, gentle voice, but Fiona recognised that the invitation had a false ring to it.

'This is Stephen's celebration,' she said, managing to look him straight in the eye. 'If and when James and I have something to celebrate it'll be a good excuse for another evening out.'

Stephen smiled easily. Did he recognise Fiona's challenge? What is Anna Krohne to you? she was asking, and shouldn't the double celebration be your engagement? But she learned nothing from his expression. He might as easily have been laughing at her, mocking her, or was it the effect of the wine?

At that moment Patsy disgraced herself with a loud hiccup and Fiona was grateful that the attention was diverted from herself. Her cheeks were flushed. Some might think it was with pleasure, she hoped, but she alone knew it was over-indulgence in food and wine, while beneath the exterior her blood bubbled through her veins with catastrophic desolation. Anna Krohne was everything Fiona wasn't. A complete woman, young, beautiful, with a careless abandon which made her good company. A perfect stepmother to Stephen's children and eminently suitable to give him more. Fiona's spirits began to sag as the effects of the wine wore off, and she was glad when James decided they were all fit enough to drive home.

Laura was unnaturally chatty, and then Fiona was alone with James.

'Guess we ought to take Cass through the woods,' he laughed as she unlocked the door and switched off the burglar alarm. 'Not for her benefit, but ours.'

'I just want to fall into bed,' Fiona said.

'Is that an invitation?'

'You know me better than that, James,' she replied tartly.

'I can't go on waiting, darling. I'm only human for God's sake.'

She saw then the fire of wanting in his eyes. But was it wanting *her*, or would just any woman do?

'Good night, James. It was a lovely dinner party,' she said, a hint of dismissal in her tone.

'I need you, Fiona,' he whispered huskily. 'We should have had something to celebrate tonight, shouldn't we?'

'This was a special occasion for Stephen and the practice, I understood. Not much special about it for poor Dr Locke though.'

James sighed as he paced the floor. 'We all have to come to retirement sooner or later, Fiona. I'm sorry it took a stroke to make your idol realise he wasn't indispensable, but when I saw him a couple of days ago he was improving, and determined to regain some of his faculties. I'm sorry you aren't happy about Stephen coming into the practice permanently, but Dr and Mrs Locke are delighted.'

She hadn't said she wasn't happy about the arrangement. Was she *that* obvious?

'Would you like more coffee?' she asked changing the subject.

'No, it's past your bedtime even if it is Saturday tomorrow.'

'I need to keep in touch with the Cravens, and I'd like to visit Mrs Hartnell either tomorrow or Sunday as well as visiting Dr Locke.'

'I'm on call tomorrow, but I'll be in touch either in the evening or on Sunday.' He hugged her suddenly, and although her body melted into his embrace her inner self shrank into a tight unyielding ball.

'You're all tensed up, Fiona,' James said soothingly. 'Don't let work and all the pressures of it take you over. You've got Patsy, delegate a bit more for your own good.'

Fiona pulled away from him. 'Guess I'm just tired. It is the end of the week after all.'

Next morning Fiona went into her office as it was her turn to be on hand in case of need, but her telephone remained silent which gave her the chance to get on with all the paperwork which had accumulated. Emergency calls for a doctor were usually diverted to the private number of whichever one was on call so she was more than a little startled when the door opened and Stephen walked briskly in.

'Do you usually work at weekends?' he asked.

'Sometimes. It's a quiet time to get things sorted out. Patsy's off this weekend.'

'I thought the weekend might be a good time to visit the Abilenes up at Sykes Hill. My parents and Anna have taken the children shopping, and they're having lunch in Gorton so I have a few hours free.'

'You ducked the shopping?' she quipped easily without thinking, remembering how he had always hated busy towns and shops.

'Yes, but I won't be able to duck the bills,' he replied with a smile. Fiona was quick to notice that he looked less strained than when he had first come back to Kenelm. The arrival of Anna was responsible for that she supposed, and the laughter lines which were evident at the corners of his eyes.

He leaned over the desk and in a low appealing voice said, 'I wanted to apologise, Fiona. I didn't mean to offend you last evening by calling you "regal". I meant to imply that the beautiful royal blue dress was suitable for a princess.'

'I wasn't offended, Stephen.' She only glanced up briefly. She couldn't bear to be this close to him knowing that he saw her now only as a colleague.

'It was a good evening and that dress was really something. You always did have impeccable taste.'

'At a price, where that dress was concerned,' she laughed.

'An exclusive obviously. You know most women at over thirty are beginning to thicken, at least round the hips and waist, but there's hardly anything of you. What's your secret?'

Fiona felt her eyes burning uncomfortably.

'No secret,' she said offhandedly, wishing he would go away and analyse Anna Krohne instead. 'I eat well—over-eat I expect—but Cass keeps me in good shape.'

'You always had a good figure, but I remembered you as being a little more—rounded.' He illustrated his meaning with his hands.

'Thanks for the compliment.'

'Don't mention it,' he quipped with a twinkle of

merriment in his eyes. 'You'll soon fill out when you and James get married, and you start a family.'

'I don't know that I want one,' she said, suddenly extremely annoyed at the way the conversation was heading.

'Well if you don't hurry up it'll be too late.'

'Then I'll probably stay childless—*and* single,' she retorted. 'Though what it's got to do with you I can't imagine.'

'Everything, Fiona. Because eleven years ago we meant everything to each other, and I went away believing you had found happiness. You obviously hadn't, and frankly it puzzles me.'

'But *you* did find happiness, and you have memories too, so hang on to those.'

'I have memories, Fiona, some very special ones,' he answered slowly, then with a strangled groan he straightened up. 'I'll go and see the Abilenes.'

Fiona covered her face with her hands after the door had closed firmly behind him. He was sniffing for answers again. She had hated the secrecy and deceit eleven years ago, but now it seemed even more unbearable. Being with him again meant that one day in a fit of pique she would reveal the truth, and that must never happen. Things had turned out well for Stephen until the death of his wife, but he did have his children—he had everything to live for while she was the one who only had memories.

She knew she must soon make a decision. It was wrong of her to string James along. Deceit was becoming too easy, her hallmark, and she despised herself for it. She would have to leave Kenelm, of course, and that would really distress her. Soon she must be frank with James, then two weeks up north with her parents, maybe time to see what the job situation was like in Selkirk. She dared not believe that fate would be on her side, and she couldn't afford to be out of work. If she married James she wouldn't need to worry any more, but that was a mean suggestion, quite uncharacteristic of her. Yet she knew that she couldn't reject James and still stay on at the health centre. With a heavy heart she made some black coffee, worked on for a further hour and then drove home. There was nothing urgent which couldn't wait until Monday so she had a snack, went for a long walk through the forest with Cass, stretched out on her settee and had a nice long sleep before telephoning her parents. They were delighted, as always, to hear her voice and very pleased at her proposed visit, even though she couldn't be specific about the date.

'In two maybe three weeks,' she said, not committing herself. 'Did you have plans? If you do I can put it off.'

'No, my dear,' her mother said. 'You know we want you to come up to see us. Christmas was ages ago.'

'You could always come south,' Fiona suggested with a laugh.

'Not during the summer, Fiona. Your father doesn't like travelling much these days, especially when it gets hot and there's more traffic on the roads. He loves his home, he just wishes you were here too.'

'Well I will be soon, Mum, I promise, but you know what my job is like. I get so involved. I've been working this morning.'

'Then it's time you had a break, dear. How's James? Couldn't you both come?'

'He's on call today. He's too dedicated to take holidays.' She hurried on quickly to explain about the previous evening's dinner party, though careful not to reveal the new partner's name. She would tell them, of course, but she would save that piece of news for when she went home then they would understand her need to move on to pastures new. Once she had started running —was that how she would spend the rest of her life?

As the weekend progressed Fiona began to unwind. James telephoned with vague excuses for not seeing her until Sunday and Fiona felt relieved. She went to church on Sunday morning and after the service the vicar caught her arm.

'Fiona, I thought you'd like to know that Mr and Mrs Craven have taken Cathy abroad for a holiday; Ibiza, I believe. It all happened in a hurry, but Mrs Craven sounded quite excited on the phone.'

'It'll do them all good. I was going to call in on them tomorrow. How long will they be away?'

'She didn't say, but if I hear anything I'll let you know. Oh, and there's Mrs Hartnell, but I expect you know about that?'

'Yes, I'm hoping to visit her today, and Dr Locke too.'

'You should be out enjoying this lovely weather, Fiona. Isn't it time you had a holiday?' the vicar said.

'I'm hoping to do just that in two or three weeks' time. It'll be nice to see my parents again.'

Fiona was puzzled by his interest. He'd never shown any curiosity before about her private life, as although she liked and admired him for his dedication to his pastoral work they only came in contact over people of Kenelm in trouble. As she drove home she wondered how naive she was being. Eleven years was a considerable time to allow people to forget the past, but in a smallish community rumour ran riot and she supposed tongues had started wagging. Stephen was becoming a familiar figure now in the district, and no doubt the middle-aged to elderly could take pleasure in connecting the past and the present. Fiona was too busy trying to redirect her future. She must make up her mind, she told herself firmly, and wouldn't it be better to go home to her parents for a while? They needed her companionship now in their twilight years and she desperately needed to change course, to be somewhere where the past could be buried and she could become involved in new people and places.

But Stephen would always be with her no matter how far away she went. Why should she cut loose from any connections? Was she strong enough to stand firm, love him from afar and watch him go into his future with a young, healthy woman?

CHAPTER ELEVEN

SUMMER promised to be long and sultry, bringing as always numerous minor complaints from rashes, tummy upsets, babies restless at night, to the elderly unable to cope, and Fiona and Patsy were always on the go as their advice was sought after. Fiona said nothing to James about her proposed holiday, and because of the work load at the practice she and Stephen treated each other with mutual respect, hardly having time for anything more than discussions about patients. Fiona kept putting off her visit to her parents. As long as she could keep up this level of pretence, however difficult, she decided to keep going, and the need to move on became less important.

She was packing up early one evening as the local dancing school were putting on their summer show in the village hall, and Fiona, known to almost all of the children and their parents, was given a complimentary ticket. She felt hot and sticky and was anxious to get home to shower and change in good time, but as she walked down the corridor towards the stairs she met Stephen coming up.

'Ah, glad I've caught you,' he said.

'Well, I am in a hurry, Stephen. I'm going to the dancing school's show this evening.'

'This is much more important. Can we go back into your office?' He grabbed her bare arm, turned her round, and propelled her along the corridor.

'It'll have to be quick,' she said as she unlocked the

door. 'I'm later now than I intended.'

'The Abilenes,' he said, with a touch of impatience.

'What about them?'

'Can't *you* make them see sense? I've been up there three times, and all I get is abuse from the husband. I'm sure the girl could be talked round.'

'Then you're the right one to do it, aren't you?'

'What's that supposed to mean?' he snapped. 'Sarcasm about my non-existent charm?'

'Oh, Stephen,' Fiona said in an imploring voice. 'You know I didn't mean to be sarcastic. Maybe if you and Meggie agreed to Mrs Abilene having a home confinement provided you're informed the moment she goes into labour you'd win them round that way.'

Stephen brushed his hair back with his hands. He was hot and sticky as well. Although he wasn't wearing a jacket he was still dressed immaculately in dark brown trousers, an apricot coloured shirt and matching striped tie, and Fiona could feel and smell the maleness of him. He was an intense person when faced with an insoluble problem, and he hated defeat.

'There's more to this than bloody-mindedness,' he mused thoughtfully. 'Mr Abilene actually blames the health care services for the death of his mother. Too many technicians and tests, he says, instead of allowing nature to take its course. She was induced, from what I gather. The baby survived, but his mother died. I suspect there were complications, but how can you argue when you don't know the case history? We've got to make them see sense somehow, Fiona.'

'I'll visit again, but if we make too much of a nuisance of ourselves it'll only make them more determined. Meggie's the one who should try to win their confidence.'

'But the very fact that she wears a uniform could be off-putting. Will you go again soon, Fiona? At least try to get her to have a blood sample taken for cross-matching?'

'I don't think it'll be of any use, but I'll go if I'm up that way—now, I must fly.'

Stephen's face cleared as if the Abilenes' problem faded as he realised that Fiona was in a hurry.

'A show did you say?'

She patiently repeated details of the concert.

'Couldn't I come too? I mean, bring the kids? Just the sort of thing they'd love, and I want you to meet my family, Fiona.'

There was such pleading in his voice that Fiona instantly weakened. 'I expect the tickets have all been sold for both evenings, but if I agree to stand they might make room for the children.'

'Just the two girls, Rebecca and Nicola,' he said. 'Andrew's only three, and he'd get bored anyway. It'll give me a chance to show my interest in the local goings-on.'

'I think *you* may well be bored,' she countered with a smile.

He shook his head. 'Don't think so. The girls will want to join the dancing school, I expect. I'm a dab-hand at following children's pursuits since Martha died. There's nothing like having a family of your own to learn to understand the problems we encounter in our work. Where's the show being held?'

'The village hall. Seven o'clock—it's early because of the tinies who take part. They'll perform in the first half so that they can go home if they're tired. You could always take yours home at the interval,' she suggested.

'I doubt if Becky or Niki would allow that. They're

eight and five respectively—no, they'll insist on staying to the end.'

'They've settled down in England with no problems?'

Stephen rubbed his jaw with a nervous gesture. 'No one can take their mother's place and the two girls are old enough to remember, but Andrew has forgotten. Grandmas and nannies fill a need, but—it can never be the same.' He walked stiffly to the window. Poor darling, Fiona thought, if only there was something she could do to make up for his loss. To see him hurt and unhappy caused her pain too, but she realised she couldn't possibly bridge the gap his wife's death had left.

'Right then, we'll meet at the village hall at about a quarter to seven.' He faced her squarely. 'Should I ring whoever's in charge, buy some tickets, make a donation?'

'All the money in the world won't buy vacant seats if there aren't any, but I'll ring Katie and see what she suggests.'

'*Our* Katie? Katie, the canteen lady?'

'That's right, Katie the cleaner, cook, mother of five children, and professional dance teacher. Don't ask me how she manages it all, but she thrives on hard work. She's hyperactive. Her eldest daughter of fifteen helps her run the dancing school with another friend of Katie's, and they teach to an excellent standard.'

Stephen opened the door and allowed Fiona to pass through first, closing it behind her. He gave her a friendly tap on her shoulder as he strode away leaving her trembling slightly, her fingers shaky as she tried to push the key into the lock. She paused for several seconds to regain some composure before going downstairs. He didn't really deserve any pity she decided. His children, yes, but was Anna Krohne the right person to take their mother's place? Fiona had to admit that she had the right kind of personality which would readily accept a family of three children. She was young and vivacious, capable of making Stephen happy and adding to his family.

When she reached home Fiona didn't have enough time to prepare a meal so she ate a couple of crispbreads topped with cheese, and afterwards munched an apple as she opened drawers and her wardrobe trying to decide what to wear. A simple cotton sun dress had been put ready but now in her subconscious mind she felt the need to compete with the lovely Anna.

After her shower and shampoo she blow dried and styled her honey-coloured hair. Maybe she would go to the hairdresser one day and have her hair bleached to platinum blonde, but somehow it didn't appeal to her. Her hair was naturally shaded, soft and silky with loose waves. You're as you are, she told her reflection, and it's useless to compete with the Swedish beauty. At least she must make an effort to look as attractive as possible, so she chose a multi-coloured floral silk skirt with matching loose waistcoat and a frilly cream georgette blouse. White high-heeled sandals and a small shoulder bag completed her outfit, and as she met her twin in the long wardrobe mirror she appraised herself as looking reasonably good. You're only thirty-two she admonished, a lifetime ahead in which to keep yourself this way.

She was too late to catch Katie at home so she drove with all speed to the village hall, parked her car and went back stage where she found her as always, cool and calm despite the score of small children in the process of being dressed by their mums in a variety of costumes.

'Are you sold out for this evening, Katie?' Fiona asked.

'Yes, thank goodness, but what a time to pick to ask, or is there a particular reason?'

'Dr Radcliffe is coming with a friend and his two little girls. I don't mind standing as long as we can seat the two children.'

'Oh, anything for Dr Radcliffe, my dear. You'll find my eldest boy, Matthew, with his dad, helping with the seating arrangements. Tell them to put a couple of chairs along the side at the front, and two of those baby chairs in the front row. Best I can do at such short notice, but there's always the chance that someone won't turn up. Keep your eye open for empty seats once we've started.'

Katie's husband was already putting extra chairs along the wall at the side of the hall as Fiona explained what was required. 'Sure to get a few people sneaking in after it's started,' he said. 'We'll put the baby chairs right in the front and Dr Radcliffe and his friend on the side. You've got your ticket haven't you, Fiona?'

'Yes, I'm always half way down on the other side near the door in case of any accidents. Unofficial first-aider,' she laughed.

Katie's husband put reserved tickets on the newly arranged chairs and Fiona went outside. In the lobby her attention was drawn to two little girls with jet black hair, round faces and beautiful dark eyes, of Asian origin without doubt. When Stephen's voice rang out, 'Oh, here she is' to the person demanding his ticket, Fiona could only stare from him to the children.

'Well,' he demanded crisply, 'are we allowed in or not?'

Fiona blinked in response. 'Yes, yes, they've put out some extra chairs. It's okay, Doris,' she said to the lady at the table. 'Dr Radcliffe is sort of guest of honour.'

'We'll pay for our seats the same as everyone else

though,' Stephen said, suddenly smiling, and taking out a crisp ten-pound note pushed it into Doris' hand. 'Putting on a show must cost money so put that in the kitty.'

Fiona walked away from the table and Stephen followed, one of the little Asian girls on each side.

'This is Fiona,' he explained to them, and to Fiona, 'This is Becky, and the little one is Niki.' A hint of amusement crossed his face then as he saw Fiona's look of utter astonishment.

'Maybe no one told you,' he whispered, 'my wife was Indonesian.'

'No,' Fiona said, still in a state of shock, 'I didn't know.'

Stephen stood close to Fiona and looking directly into her face said softly, 'She was brought up in New Zealand from a child but qualified as a doctor in the States before going back to Australia to practise.'

'You must be very proud of your children, Stephen. They're quite adorable.'

'I'm glad you think so.' Then his face wrinkled into a thousand creases. 'I don't always when they're behaving badly, which they do frequently—and being girls they try to put the blame on Andrew.'

Fiona suspected that he was besotted with his children, but mostly the three-year-old boy.

'You didn't bring Anna?' Fiona asked, looking over his shoulder.

'No, how could I? She's looking after Andy.'

Fiona had imagined that his mother might have been doing that, but evidently Anna was already acting as the children's mother.

'I'll show you to your seats,' she said, and led the way into the small hall, and down the side. 'I hope this is all right, Stephen. They were fully booked up for tonight and tomorrow night. I kept two seats for you in case——' her voice trailed off as she bent to pick up the spare reserved ticket.

Stephen grabbed her arm painfully. 'Anna is the children's nanny,' he said pointedly. 'A fully qualified nursery nurse who came over here with me from Australia. I only invited her to be my guest at the dinner because——' he stopped as abruptly as he'd begun. 'Because I didn't want to be the odd one out without a partner, or teamed up with Laura—or—or—Patsy,' he finished with impatience.

Fiona's mind was a maze of thoughts running in every direction but she managed to say, 'Will the children be all right in the front? Not far away from you?'

He nodded and guided the two little girls to the small chairs.

'You're very lucky to be given front seats,' he told them. 'Now, don't let me down. Sit still and be good.'

Fiona smiled at their eager expressions. 'I'll leave you to it then,' she said.

'What d'you mean?' Stephen demanded, panic-stricken.

'I usually sit on the opposite side of the hall near the door in case anyone is taken ill. I'm on first-aid duty.'

'Then they can come over here for you if they want you. For God's sake don't leave me here on my own with all these women and children.'

Fiona laughed aloud. 'I know it sounds a bit rowdy at the moment, but it'll be okay once they get started.'

'You sit right here with me.'

Fiona pursed her lips doubtfully. 'We-ell, I'd better go to tell them, and I'll get some programmes.'

The hall was filling rapidly, an air of excitement

pervading as relatives and friends of the children performing eagerly awaited the beginning of the annual
concert. Fiona told Katie's husband that the chair reserved for her would now be vacant, then she fought her
way back to where Stephen was sitting looking somewhat out of place. She remembered trying to get James
to accompany her to watch the local children performing
a year ago, but he had declined very definitely. He didn't
have children of his own, but Stephen had two of the
most endearing little girls she had ever seen. His mother
must be in her element with them and then Fiona
remembered seeing photos of Asian children at the
house when Stephen had taken her there after rushing
Cathy to hospital. Because of their appealing looks
Fiona had noticed the photographs, but in her subconscious had registered that they were probably orphan
children whom Stephen's eldest sister, Margaret, had
dealt with in the course of her work as a missionary. It
had never crossed her mind that they could be Stephen's
family. She searched her memory trying to recall if there
had been a photograph of an Asian woman, but her
memory and her imagination fused together exploding
into nothing of significance as the music began, and the
children in their delightful innocent way started their
performance. Fiona's spirits began to lift. Anna was in
Stephen's employ as the children's nanny. Stephen
wasn't yet committed to anyone else. Oh, she shouldn't
have been jealous, she *mustn't* be jealous, and yet she
felt a sense of contentment that he was free, even though
she knew it couldn't affect her in the slightest.

Soon they were laughing and applauding with the rest
of the audience. Becky and Niki joining in with wide
eyes full of contentment. At the interval Stephen asked
Fiona to take them to the ladies' room while he procured

ice-creams for them all.

'Martha wouldn't have approved,' Stephen said softly. 'She disliked them eating out between meals, but they can't be excluded from having fun like the rest of the company.'

'They're certainly enjoying it,' Fiona agreed.

When the final curtain came down to a well-pleased audience Stephen held on to the children as he turned to Fiona.

'You'll come back to the house, of course?'

'Thanks, but no, Stephen.' Her cold refusal came unbidden, sounding hurtful. She hadn't anticipated being asked. There was no reason why she shouldn't accept and in her heart it was what she wanted, but when Stephen replied gruffly, 'I suppose James will be expecting you,' she realised her mistake.

'It is quite late,' she said quickly.

Stephen's mouth was set in a hard line. 'Thanks very much for getting us in. I must see Katie about the girls starting at the dancing school in the autumn.'

There was no opportunity for further conversation as they got pushed in all directions trying to get to the door of the hall. Fiona's attention was claimed by one of her young mums, and the last she saw of Stephen was in the distance towering above everyone else as he passed through the doorway with his youngest daughter in his arms.

It was much later as she pulled into her drive that she found her eyes filling with tears. Tears for Stephen, and the delightful children who had been so cruelly robbed of their mother, as well as tears for herself. She was in a dilemma, half of her knowing that she was throwing away her chance of happiness with James, while the other half of her yearned for what had been within her grasp eleven years ago. But she couldn't dwell on the past. She had done what she believed to be right at the time, however much it had cost her. Stephen had reaped his reward and his harvest was a lasting one steeped in love for his children. She felt that he would probably never marry again for no one could compare with a woman of grace and charm from Indonesia which Martha must have been to bear Stephen such lovely children.

Cass greeted Fiona affectionately and barked as soon as she took down her lead from the hook.

'You don't let up, do you?' she grumbled good-naturedly. 'Expect you're right, Cass, a bit of exercise will work off the melancholy.' She smiled as she locked her door. What would people think if they could hear her rabbiting on to a dog! In the event she didn't walk far as she had forgotten to change her shoes to flatties, but it was a perfect, still summer evening; the sun was only just beginning to reluctantly sink in the west, and holidaymakers were ambling through the forest walks making the most of the last of the daylight. As she turned back along the pathway towards the camp site she could smell charcoal burning. A barbecue party was in full swing in the area provided, and Fiona's steps quickened towards home as she responded to the aroma of steak and sausages, realising how hungry she was.

'What shall we have, Cass?' she said as she went into her kitchen. 'I know, liver and onions—we aren't socialising again tonight.'

A male laugh echoed behind her from the doorway. 'You really do have the most peculiar tastes still.'

'Stephen!' Fiona swung round, her cheeks scarlet with embarrassment that she had been overheard.

'Enough for two?' he asked with a wicked grin.

'I . . . I thought . . . well, yes, if you haven't eaten, I suppose.'

'I wouldn't be cadging off you if I had. I was just about to leave. I decided you must have gone to James' flat.'

Fiona turned her back on him. 'We don't live in each other's pockets,' she said candidly, and glancing at him noticed that he raised his eyebrows quizzically.

'I was in trouble for not taking you home to supper, then I realised that perhaps I'd been hasty in supposing you were seeing James. I should have thanked you, Fiona, for arranging entry to the show. You made two little girls blissfully happy. Becky can't understand why her shoes don't tap on the kitchen floor.'

'All little girls dream of being able to dance.'

'And most big girls dream of dancing with their idol too. We were pretty good on the dance floor, I seem to remember.'

'That was all a long time ago in our youth, Stephen.'

'And we're past all that, I suppose?' He took a few steps farther into the kitchen. Fiona sensed that he wanted to touch her so she quickly went to the fridge-freezer in an effort to stall him, knowing that she couldn't trust herself.

'Were you serious about the liver and onions?' she asked brightly.

'Of course—sounds delicious.'

As she peeled the onions and tossed them into the hot fat she remembered the steak she had saved for such a night as this. No, she mentally argued, steak was too good for this casual supper. Steak was for celebrating and she didn't consider she had anything to celebrate. Maybe when she made up her mind and finally left Kenelm she would invite Stephen and James to enjoy the steak as a farewell gesture—but that wouldn't exactly be celebrating, she thought, a cold draught of misery wafting over her.

'It's rather late to be eating fried onions, isn't it?' she suggested lightly.

'As you told Cass, we aren't socialising again tonight and ten o'clock isn't that late—not too late to talk about the Abilenes, I hope?'

Fiona stifled a sigh. So that was it, she might have known. He hadn't come to see her, to thank her for getting the children into the show, or to talk about the past—work was always uppermost in his mind. No wonder his marriage to a doctor had worked. A nanny for the children, giving his wife time to share in his one and only love. There had been a time when she had been glad to share in that love, and then she had held the secret of being able to cleverly steer the conversation round to other things at just the right moment. Now, alone with him she felt just a wee bit excited, and a tiny bit nervous, and reckoned that to talk about their patients was probably the safest avenue of discussion.

'Hasn't it all been said?'

'Where's your fighting spirit? You know we can't let her have that baby all up there with only her husband in attendance.'

'It's still a free country, isn't it?'

'That's the easy option. You know better than that, Fiona. Would you let your husband dictate to you as to where you'd have your baby?'

It was as if an arrow had pierced her heart, aiming for and hitting the bull's eye.

'That's a hypothetical question,' she answered softly as she turned the liver and onions over in the pan. 'Oh,' she added quickly, 'I haven't done potatoes or chips.'

'No need. I'm sure you've got a crust of bread.'

'Stephen,' she said solemnly, 'this isn't going to be much of a meal. It was only meant for me and Cass.'

'Are you trying to get rid of me?'

'No, but——'

'But nothing—hurry up, the smell is driving me wild.'

The way to a man's heart, she thought cynically as she took two plates down from the grill. 'The bread is over there in the bread bin, and the butter's on the table.'

He reacted instantly while Fiona set out two place mats and knives and forks on the pine-wood table in the kitchen. She was sure he wasn't used to eating in the kitchen so this would ensure that he wouldn't invite himself again, but she felt the atmosphere becoming cosy as they sat opposite one another eating in silence while Cass relished her helping with noisy appreciation.

'Fiona, I don't want to embarrass you,' Stephen said on a rush of expectant breath.

'Why should you?'

'Mother says that I might be making things awkward between you and James.'

'How's that?' She was deliberately obtuse.

'Working all together can't be helped,' he said, 'but going to the concert tonight—did it look—sort of—fixed?'

'Stephen, what are you trying to say?'

'That I'm sorry if I put you on the spot. I hoped James would understand.'

Fiona laughed. 'James wouldn't have gone to the show, if that's what you mean, and I'm sure he'd understand that you wanted to take your little girls.'

'But he might think Anna could have gone with them. The truth is—never mind, it's done with now,' he finished decisively, then as he laid aside his knife and fork he added, 'Martha—you haven't asked about

Martha—she caught a rare virus and this seemed to trigger off a blood disorder. Coming so soon after Andrew's birth—she had him at home you see—well, all the children because we lived in a remote area, but there was a midwife who attended when the girls were born. I know it's silly, Fiona, but I feel that I may have failed Martha. She should have been in hospital, but she had similar ideas to the Abilenes. Of course, she had all the relevant tests during her pregnancies but she wasn't too well during the last one, then when the time came the midwife was attending another case so I delivered Martha of Andrew. In a way that's why he's so special to me now, but I can't rid myself of a certain feeling of guilt.'

He covered his face with his hands. Was this the first time he had voiced his fears to anyone? Why had he chosen Fiona to confide in? Didn't he realise she too had a guilt complex? No, he didn't and her secret must be kept locked away in the confines of her mind.

'I'm sure you did everything you could for your wife, Stephen,' she assured him. 'I doubt if her death had anything at all to do with the last confinement. That's just coincidence—it happens all the time. People speculate, put two and two together and make five. Surely you were able to get the facts in the end?'

He rubbed his cheeks vigorously. 'Yes, and I know in my heart that there was no connection, nor was there anything anyone could do. I'm sorry, Fiona, I shouldn't have burdened you with this, but I felt you'd understand —after all, it's your job to listen. Sometimes I feel bitter about Martha's death. She was a brilliant paediatrician with so much experience and knowledge to offer to society. Why, Fiona, *why*?'

Fiona felt a lump in her throat. What did he expect her to say?

'Isn't that the kind of question you should ask the vicar?'

Stephen looked up at her aggressively. 'Don't send me up, Fiona. I did think you'd have some compassion.'

'I'm *not* sending you up,' she denied indignantly, 'but you're asking me impossible questions. Of course I feel compassion for anyone in your situation, but being bitter and twisted about it won't bring her back.'

He looked again at her, his expression one of disappointment. What do you want of me? Fiona pleaded silently. Stephen bent his head, and Fiona excused herself and went to the sink to fill the kettle.

'Tea or coffee?' she asked presently.

'It's late now. I'm sorry, my dear Fiona, I've used you in a disgraceful way. Please forgive me and apologise to James, I have no right to be here. I have no right to expect you to be interested in Martha or the children. . Why the hell should you be expected to listen to my sob story? No, Fiona, I'm not really bitter and twisted, nor am I riddled with self pity even if it does appear that way—it's the children who've been cheated, and I find that hard to take.'

'Your children have you, Stephen—isn't that what matters?'

Stephen stood up, faced Fiona as she stood with her back to the sink, and bent to kiss her tenderly. 'Thanks,' he said hoarsely, 'for the best meal I've had in weeks, and for—just being here.' He almost ran out of her mobile home. Mobile she wished it was, the sort where you could just start the engine and take off. To where was unimportant, but already her thoughts were travelling ahead of her northwards to her parents where she could unburden her grief. She knew now that to stay in Kenelm would cause her nothing but more pain. Stephen was grieving for Martha . . .

CHAPTER TWELVE

Fiona didn't get as far as the Abilenes before the weekend. She hoped 'no news meant good news' and promised herself that they would be first on the list on Monday morning. Stephen's visit to her home after the concert left her feeling fatigued, and yet she continued to put her patients before arranging her holiday. She couldn't just up and off when people needed her, she argued, and now that Mrs Hartnell was back in her own home again Fiona felt it necessary to call on her each day, even at weekends.

On Saturday afternoon she put James off by saying that her garden needed attention, and she put all her energy into watering, weeding, feeding and mowing the lawn, then on Sunday she felt too tired to get up and go to church, but later in the day she went to visit Dr and Mrs Locke. It was early afternoon, a hot, breathless kind of day when even a sleeveless, thin cotton dress seemed almost too much to wear, and the heat inside the car was unbearable so Cassie was left at home in the coolest bedroom.

Mrs Locke answered the door and welcomed Fiona with a happy smile.

'My dear, I was thrilled when you rang, but you should have come to lunch. Esmond is so looking forward to seeing you. This past month has seen a great improvement.'

'I wondered how the heat would affect him,' Fiona said.

'It seems to be doing him good. It isn't as if he's very active you see, so it doesn't tire him, and of course he can only sustain anything for a short while, then he has to rest.'

'I won't stay long then as I expect he's having an afternoon nap.'

'He made sure he had that before you arrived, Fiona. Come along through to the front sitting-room. The sun is at the back of the house at this time of day so it's cooler in here.'

The room was light and airy without any direct sunlight and Fiona sank into one of the easy chairs close to where Dr Locke was sitting. Soon they were engrossed in conversation, Fiona being required to give a detailed account of all Kenelm's activities as well as the health of Dr Locke's patients, and future plans for the health centre.

'I'm going to be well again, Fiona,' he laughed, and she was delighted that he could speak intelligibly again. 'I know I'll never be able to put in a full day's work, not even half a day perhaps, but I can help out during a heavy spell or holidays.'

Fiona smiled warmly. It did her heart good to see him on the road to recovery, and she knew that his own determination had a great deal to do with it, plus his wife's devotion and understanding.

Mrs Locke came in with a tray of tea.

'I'm sure the younger generation would think we're mad drinking tea on a hot afternoon, but I maintain it refreshes you in the long run. Fiona, I'm surprised you haven't been away on holiday during this fine weather.'

'Nothing is definite yet, Mrs Locke, but I'm planning to visit my parents up north soon.'

Both the doctor and his wife were quick to notice a

reticent tone in Fiona's voice, and she knew she couldn't fool them.

'Only a holiday? Or are things getting you down here?' Mrs Locke questioned hesitantly.

Fiona remained silent, blinking away threatened tears.

'It is awkward,' she finally admitted with a quiver in her voice.

'Drink your tea, my dear. You know Esmond and I love you all at the practice, but we are concerned that you don't become unhappy.'

'Stephen's coming seems to have created a barrier between James and myself. James knows nothing of the past yet he has cooled towards me. At the moment he appears to be helping Laura over some sort of crisis, but they don't confide in the rest of us. I know it would be wrong of me to marry James even if he wanted it which I now suspect he doesn't, so I need someone to give me a push to go up to Selkirk. Away from everyone here maybe I shall see things more clearly, and if there are job opportunities up there I shall move where I can keep an eye on my parents.'

'How do you and Stephen get on?' Dr Locke asked kindly.

Fiona explained how she had thought Anna was his new love, and how she had met his two daughters.

'I had no idea his wife was foreign,' she said.

Dr Locke studied Fiona thoughtfully. 'Sometimes, when we've been hurt, and happiness seems to have gone for ever, we look for it in a completely new area. As far as English girls go, Fiona, I feel sure that no one could ever take your place in Stephen's life. In Martha he found the complete contrast—there was nothing in her looks or culture that would remind him of you.

Colleagues at first, you see, nothing more, but with time they developed a mutual respect and admiration for one another.'

'I'm confident that he loved her very much indeed, and I feel he's trying to tell me that he'll never marry again. So—' Fiona sighed deeply, 'I'll be doing everyone a favour by leaving Kenelm. Besides, I've been here a long time—too long, I expect, and you know what they say about familiarity.'

'That will never apply to you, Fiona,' Mrs Locke said sternly. 'From your parents' point of view I know they'd love to have you up north with them, but not if your heart remains here.'

'And only you know what you feel sincerely in your heart, my dear,' the wise old doctor said with feeling. 'My advice, for what it's worth, is to let things run a natural course, but of one thing I am certain, and that is that you need a holiday.'

Fiona loved them for their honesty, and was grateful to have two such kind friends with whom she could be honest too. It wasn't so much what she revealed in dialogue, but they knew her well enough to sense her confusion and misery.

A couple of hours later she reached home a few minutes after James had arrived.

'Thought you'd deserted me,' he said grinning broadly.

'Only for Dr and Mrs Locke. I've been so busy of late I haven't had time to visit them, but I've kept in touch by phone. It's quite incredible how that dear man has fought back.'

James agreed, and while he fetched garden chairs from the shed, Fiona prepared tall glasses of iced fruit juice, and any awkwardness quickly dissolved as they relaxed in the sun with Cassie stretched out under the shade of the patio umbrella.

It was only much later, after a meal out and a walk by the river, when Fiona was alone again, lying naked on her bed, allowing the merest hint of a breeze to waft lazily over her body, that she looked back and realised how she had refrained from any mention of Stephen, and James had carefully avoided the merest hint of Laura's name.

They were back to being good friends again and Fiona knew that in her deepest thoughts that was all she really wanted. Stephen was so right when he'd said that she wasn't being fair to James; she just wished it hadn't been Stephen who'd said it. The day had been more pleasant than she'd expected and now, after talking to Dr and Mrs Locke she felt that she must let her life drift along without attempting to make decisions as yet.

Her body reacted spontaneously as the light breeze quickened with the night darkness. Her skin felt silky and cool to her touch, and as her fingers slid down her thighs she experienced shivers of sensuality as memories of nights such as this eleven years ago had brought an awakening of passion between herself and Stephen. He had been an exciting man then, eager and skilful in helping her to shed shy inhibitions. Now he was fully matured, still as handsome as ever, but with a sad aura around him. Change had overtaken them both, and even though outwardly her physical form hadn't altered, inside she was missing the vital part of her that craved to be fulfilled. Marriage was designed for pro-creation, she would never be able to fulfil her duty to any man in that direction, whereas Stephen's pathway had changed course, and he had enjoyed the peak of completeness.

She rolled over into a ball, pulled a sheet over her and refused to imagine what might have been if only . . .

Fiona slapped the top of her alarm clock, but the bell refused to be silenced, and Cassie barked furiously. It was still dark and she had been in a deep sleep, so it took several seconds to locate the bell to the telephone. She fumbled, and moaned with annoyance until at last she found the light switch and then in a husky voice she answered the telephone.

'Miss Meredith, can you come?' a masculine voice implored in panic. 'Please—*hurry*! I've delivered the baby, but Jenny is bleeding.'

Fiona was instantly awake and knew at once who was speaking.

'All right, Mr Abilene, keep calm, get the end of the bed up on some bricks or blocks, I'll be with you shortly.' She all but fell off the bed and groped about in a stupor, pulling on underwear and a pair of navy blue cotton trousers and a white tee-shirt. By the time she was dressed her brain was functioning reasonably well and she went through to her kitchen and looked at the copy of the duty rosta hanging on the wall.

Laura was on call and by the speed with which she answered her telephone Fiona decided she must be either a very light sleeper or had been prevented from sleep by previous calls.

'Sykes Hill—yes, farther on than the gypsies. I'll see you there,' Laura said.

Lights streaming out from the cottage urged Fiona forward and at the gateway she ignored the 'No cars beyond this point' sign, and pulled up sharply at the cottage door. Owen Abilene practically pulled her inside. 'It came early, it's tiny—will it be all right?'

'I hope for your sake, Mr Abilene, that both mother and baby *are* all right!' It was unlike Fiona to be short with anyone, but wasn't this just what Perry had predicted? At a moment's notice everyone had to drop everything and were expected to know exactly what to do with little or no information to go on.

Fiona observed the situation in a flash, and by the look of relief on Mrs Abilene's face she guessed that the bleeding was due to the stress of not having a doctor or midwife present rather than to any physical complication. Within a few minutes Laura followed her in and while Fiona attended to the baby Mrs Abilene was given an injection to stem the bleeding.

'You won't send me to hospital will you?' Mrs Abilene pleaded.

'I haven't decided yet,' Laura said. 'I understand you've had no ante-natal care, let alone tests, so we don't even have a blood group. This could all be taken care of much quicker in Gorton hospital.'

'But I don't believe in blood transfusions.'

'Definitely no blood transfusion,' Owen Abilene said firmly from the doorway. 'There's too much risk.'

'Many people are alive today because someone donated a pint of blood,' Laura retorted.

'And there's quite a few people who have died from viruses attributed to bottled blood,' Owen argued.

'Right now I'm concerned with how best to treat your wife,' Laura said. 'The bleeding has stopped and thankfully her blood pressure is much about what we'd expect after confinement.'

'I told him it would stop,' Jenny Abilene said. 'I know you must think we're pretty irresponsible, Doctor, but you must admit we haven't wasted much of your time. After all, Henry James is safely delivered, and he looks and sounds healthy enough even if he is a little less than six pounds.'

'You've actually weighed him?' Laura couldn't hide her astonishment.

'Yes. We had the scales all ready, and Owen did it while we were waiting for the placenta to come.' She smiled, the first flush of motherhood beginning to fade as an anaemic pallor became evident.

Laura hummed and aahed a few times before admitting that, the haemorrhage apart, the Abilenes had made a pretty good job of their home delivery. 'You'll need a hefty course of iron and vitamins, Mrs Abilene,' she said, 'and please—don't go it alone next time.'

'I'm grateful to you and Miss Meredith for coming so promptly, Doctor,' Owen Abilene butted in, coming to stand by his wife's bedside, 'but we'll always do it this way. My wife is registered with you, and Henry James will be, but we'll only ever call you in an emergency.'

'And *you?* If you should suddenly be taken ill?'

'We believe in natural medicines. I've made it my business to study the human body, its functions and possible malfunctions. I didn't just deliver Henry James by guesswork you know.'

'Supposing your wife had needed stitches?' Laura pursued.

'That would have been classed as an emergency, but we followed all the natural methods of relaxation and pre-natal preparation so it wasn't something we anticipated. Tribes-women in Africa don't have medical facilities on their doorstep.'

'But their lifestyle is somewhat different from ours.'

'Yours maybe.' He smiled suddenly, and Laura

recognised relief on his rugged countenance. 'Ours is as near to the wild as we can get.'

Fiona had bathed the baby but before dressing him she laid him in his mother's lap to allow Laura to check him over.

'He's bonny enough,' Laura announced, packing her stethoscope into her bag. 'Heartbeat as strong as mine which isn't bad for a mere five-pounder. I'll leave you to brief Mrs Abilene, Fiona, while I have a word with Mr Abilene.'

'Isn't he lovely, Miss Meredith?' Jenny Abilene crowed.

Fiona gazed down at the rosebud mouth and healthy pink skin. Already a chubby fist was finding its way into that rosebud mouth and Fiona felt an emptiness in the pit of her stomach that she would never know the magic experience of motherhood, and all because of some crazy 'I own the road' driver. It wasn't Stephen's fault, and one day she would have to beg him to believe that she hadn't blamed him for the accident, then or now. She dressed the baby with tender, loving gentleness, and then placed him in a shawl in his mother's arms before commencing to clear up the blood-stained towels and sheets.

'Oh no, Miss Meredith——'

'Fiona, please.'

'All right, Fiona, but *no*, definitely *no*, we didn't get you here to do the menial task of clearing up. We did this our way, as far as we were able, we're grateful to you and Dr O'Neal for coming, but Owen will insist on doing the dirty work.'

Fiona had to admire them and she said as much to Laura outside the cottage as they prepared to leave. It was a chilly dawn before the sun peeped over the horizon. 'A bit like standing on top of the world,' Fiona said, looking round and down at the countryside below with Gorton's chimneys and high-rise flats etched against the colourless sky. The voice of an occasional farm animal greeted the morning from the closer Kenelm as the first ray of weak sunshine illuminated the morning.

'Back to my place for breakfast?' Laura suggested.

'Or mine?' Fiona countered.

'I'm still on call until seven-thirty and that's a couple of hours to go so I'd better be hostess, unless you want to try to have a bit more sleep.'

Fiona shook her head and was soon following Laura's car down the hill past the gypsy encampment where some of the men were already up and doing and they waved to Fiona and Laura as they sped by. A few minutes later they pulled into the visitor's car-park at the block of flats where Laura lived.

Inside the small entrance hall Fiona began to whisper her opinion of the Abilenes.

'There's no one here, Fiona. I live on my own,' Laura said.

'Oh?' It was a question which she felt impertinent to pursue, so Laura gave a nervous laugh as she said, 'He's deserted me.'

'Laura! I'm *so* sorry—what can I say? Maybe it's only temporary.'

'It's for good,' Laura said, leading the way into her square luxurious kitchen.

'You mean divorce?'

Laura shook her head. She was standing at the sink filling the coffee percolator, and in the silence Fiona was aware of stifled sobs.

'I'm sorry, Laura, I didn't mean to sound inquisitive.

Don't talk about it if you'd rather not.'

Laura switched on the percolator and took bread out of the pine-wood bread-bin.

'Everyone will know sooner or later,' she said with a sniff. 'We weren't married, Fiona—I hope that doesn't shock you.'

'Why should it? It's the done thing these days, though I have to say it wouldn't suit me.' She laughed. 'Chance would be a fine thing anyway.'

'Oh, come on,' Laura said, turning round quickly, 'you've got James, you can't tell me that at your ages——?'

'We haven't slept together?' Fiona finished for her. 'I expect I've been a disappointment to James, but—oh dear——' Fiona took a deep breath, almost glad to have found someone in whom she could confide, 'I don't honestly love him in that way. I am very fond of him, and at one point I really began to believe we could be happy together, but now I know I was mistaken and it wouldn't be fair to James.'

'Does James know you feel like this?'

'Not yet, so please don't say anything to him yet.'

'Fiona, I wouldn't dream of discussing your feelings for him *with* him. To be a good nurse or doctor you have to be able to keep confidences, and I believe I'm quite good at it.'

'I . . . I'm thinking of going up north to see my parents so I must talk things over with James first. Patsy will be off for a couple of weeks soon, so then I shall take my holidays—but that's enough about me. Laura—I don't know what to say—you sounded so final about it, and I'm really sorry.'

'I let everyone think I was married to Paul because I thought I might not get the job here if people knew we just lived together. We wanted to have a family, but I insisted on marriage first. Paul would have been difficult to hold anyway. Travelling around like he does he meets women everywhere so I guess I have to admire him for being honest enough to say no to marriage.'

'But if he really, genuinely loved you?'

'He'd have suggested marriage at the beginning. Oh, I know what you're saying is right, Fiona. I've never been happy with the arrangement, but we had a good relationship until a month or so ago. I don't know how I'd have coped without James. It's no joke suddenly getting home one night to discover your partner has up and left, bag and baggage, without so much as a thanks for the memory. James has been wonderful. I felt guilty at monopolising him when he should have been with you. I've wanted to talk to you for ages, but I thought you'd get the wrong end of the stick, and anyway, I suppose I imagined Paul would come rushing back to me.'

'James is a lovely person. He deserves happiness without being used,' Fiona said thoughtfully with a hint of guilt.

Laura poured coffee and buttered the toast. 'Let's take it into the lounge,' she suggested. 'We might as well relax. Thank goodness the Abilenes' home delivery went off without a crisis. Henry James! Poor little devil—Henry James,' she repeated slowly, 'I ask you!'

They laughed together, and after a lengthy discussion about the Abilenes Fiona remembered Cathy Craven.

'I haven't pursued it yet,' Fiona said, 'but by autumn I mean to have my help group started. We think there isn't too much of a drug problem, or solvent-sniffing problem round about here, but once you get talking to people it's surprising what you hear. Dr and Mrs Locke would be marvellous people for counselling, don't you agree?'

'I do indeed—if Dr Locke feels up to it, and I think
Stephen is an ideal candidate for the job. He's worked
abroad, Australia has a terrible drink problem I believe,
and he has a nice personality which is what is needed
most.'

'The vicar too is keen on the idea, but at present our
main concern is where to hold it. There's the church hall
or the village hall, or alternatively Lizzie's room, but I
don't know whether James would agree to that. He's
—well—not over enthusiastic about my plan. He
blames parents, and that's just what I want to get
—parents coming along to lectures and discussion
groups.'

'I can see why you've never had time to get married
and have a family, Fiona, you're too involved in the
community, but it's worth everything in a profession to
be so much respected and needed.'

Fiona sipped her coffee. Maybe it was time for
Kenelm to start getting used to being without her.
Perhaps her total commitment to the district had put
James off, or did his cooling towards her have anything
to do with Laura?

As the morning wore on Fiona began to feel the need for
sleep, yet she daren't let up as with Patsy going on
holiday soon there would only be so many visits she
could make in one day.

It was early afternoon when she went to the canteen
for something to eat.

'I've got a lovely ham salad, Fiona,' Katie told her,
producing it from a cool place. 'I was keeping it for Dr
Radcliffe, but he's evidently not coming back here from
his rounds, so I'll let you have it instead.'

'I'm not sure that I want it, Katie,' Fiona said, though

it did look appetising, and it would save her the bother of preparing a meal that evening.

'I insist, Fiona. Fancy you being called up to Sykes Hill before dawn. You look as if you could do with some sleep.'

'In the middle of the afternoon!' Stephen had come in unnoticed and stood with his arm round Fiona. 'No time for sleep, my girl, I want a full account of the Abilenes' delivery.'

Katie positively drooled at the sight of Stephen, then she pushed the ham salad along the counter to him. 'No offence, Fiona, but I did tell you I was keeping it for Dr Radcliffe.'

'That's all right, Katie,' Fiona said, wishing Katie would stop gazing mystically from her to Stephen and back again. 'I told you I didn't really want it.'

'We'll share it,' Stephen said, and by the wicked gleam in his eye he was remembering days long gone when they had only been able to afford one pot of tea and one meal to share between them during their training days.

He insisted on carrying the tray to a corner table although the canteen was empty and Katie was clearing away lunch things.

'What was it—boy or girl—and how did they cope? Had to call us in after all then?'

'Mrs Abilene was bleeding—it might have been serious if he hadn't sent for someone. It's a lovely boy —Henry James, would you believe?'

Stephen pulled a face. 'Oh, well, each to his own taste.' He pinched a piece of ham and stuffed it into his mouth.

'Stephen!' She smacked his hand sharply, and in turn he tickled her underneath her chin. They laughed together just as if the years of separation had dissolved and the slate was wiped clean. 'Look, if you want this salad then have it,' she said with light-hearted rebuff.

'I'll have a piece of that cheese,' he said, taking her hand and guiding the knife to cut the wedge in two pieces.

'You evidently didn't have any lunch,' she said.

'I did. I went home to Mother's cooking.'

'What's that supposed to mean?'

'She starves me. She's afraid I'll have a middle-age paunch.'

Fiona pointed her fork at him even though she knew it was bad-mannered. 'You always were a greedy pig,' she chided.

'But a lovable one,' he replied softly, leaning towards her and looking directly into her face.

She felt her colour rising and was grateful that at that moment the opening of the swing doors drew their attention to the arrival of James.

'What are you two up to?' He tried to make it sound frivolous, but Fiona detected a sarcastic edge to his tone.

'Stephen came for a first hand account of the Abilenes' delivery, but he's pinching my salad,' she complained.

'I came in for the same reason,' James said, then added jovially, 'to hear about the home confinement. Not your salad, darling—I'd rather have one you prepared.'

Fiona felt her cheeks getting hotter which made her a little on the defensive.

'Laura was the doctor at the Abilenes'—surely she's given you a full report, James.'

She thought he looked a little uneasy as he said, 'Yes—she's give me her version, but I understand you were the one to be called, so were there first.'

'Only by a few minutes, and Mr Abilene is quite knowledgeable. He did extremely well, but the sight of so much blood worried him which then caused Mrs Abilene some distress, but as soon as we arrived the bleeding stopped and they were quite happy. I take it Meggie will carry on visiting now whether they want her to or not?'

'And Laura too, although I daresay Mr Abilene will give them their marching orders.' James dug his hands into his pockets. 'I . . . I . . . any chance of seeing you this evening, Fiona?'

'I'm going to have an early night, James, and I won't be cooking. I daresay I shall survive on this half a salad.'

'Perhaps tomorrow evening then. I've had Mrs Craven in the surgery, but I won't bother you now. Chinese take-away tomorrow at seven?'

Stephen disentangled his long legs from beneath the chair.

'Glad everything's okay with the Abilenes,' he said abruptly, 'now it's back to the lion's den.'

He left them, Fiona finding the void almost more than she could bear, but she looked up at James with a forced smile. 'Sit down and tell me about the Cravens, James.'

He patted her back gently. 'No, my dear, you're too tired today, why don't you delegate to Patsy for the rest of the day and get off home to rest?'

'I'm not that desperate,' she said.

James raised his eyebrows, then with pursed lips he said, 'I've got surgery too, and you will be desperate for sleep by the time I get through. No, Fiona, what I want to say can wait until tomorrow. Shall I leave the meal to you then?'

'Why not? You know I like cooking, and it's more fun for two. Besides, it'll be the last you'll have for a bit if I go on holiday as soon as Patsy gets back. Is that all right with you?'

'We'll discuss it over dinner.'

He went away without another word, leaving Fiona puzzled by his seriousness. Holidays didn't have to be sanctioned by him, and she felt convinced now that she must get away—but first, yes, first she had to tell James the truth.

CHAPTER THIRTEEN

APPREHENSION prevented Fiona from concentrating too well. She attributed it to tiredness, but in her heart she was fearful of what James wanted to discuss. She felt fairly confident that anything to do with the Cravens was an excuse. She had called several times to see Cathy but found the house locked up so had assumed they were having an extra long holiday.

When she passed along the corridor on her way to her office the next morning she could hear voices and recognised them as James and Laura. She recalled the previous day's conversation with Laura and in an instant she realised that Laura was in love with James. She probably had been for some while and no doubt James felt the same way. That was what James was coming to tell her this evening. If he had needed to discuss the Cravens he would do it at the Centre—no, he needed this conversation to take place in private, and Fiona's apprehension grew. She had to admit that they were ideally suited, and she felt no hurt or jealousy, just qualms as to how James was going to tell her.

She managed to get home a little early after calling on Mrs Hartnell and finding two of her daughters there. Fiona looked guiltily at the steaks in the freezer and then on impulse decided to cook them. If this was to be the last meal with James she felt she owed him this much, and she doubted that she'd ever have the opportunity to entertain Stephen. In fact, if she was going to move on it would be wise to start running down her stock of food. A

181

fresh dairy cream lemon gâteau was just the thing for dessert. Perhaps this time James wouldn't bring a bottle of wine so she opened a carafe of rosé in readiness. She wanted everything to be as it usually was when James visited, so she selected a few choice roses in various colours, made a small arrangement on a silver salver with a pink candle in the centre. She always found James a joy to entertain, appreciative of her cooking and with an eye for the finishing touches like correct glasses and matching serviettes.

He arrived a few minutes late which was uncharacteristic of him.

'Last minute call?' Fiona asked as he kissed her gently.

'Not exactly.' He didn't elaborate further and Fiona got on with the business of dishing up.

'Mm—steak, runner beans, cauliflower and roast potatoes. What are we celebrating?' he asked.

Fiona laughed this off as she pushed a small glass of rosé into his hand.

'Try this,' she invited with a smile. There was tension in the air, and she was endeavouring to cool it by being slightly effervescent, but her voice sounded high-pitched and her laugh false.

Several times throughout the meal Fiona almost broached the subject of Laura now being on her own, as well as the Cravens, but she kept her curiosity in check. James had requested this meeting, he must be the one to do the talking.

They had reached the coffee stage. James had helped clear away and when Fiona placed the tray on the low table she said, 'I'm going to visit my parents, James. I really do feel the need for a break.'

'I should jolly well think so. Apart from the course

you went on you've not had a proper one since the Christmas holiday, and it's not so far off winter again.'

'If I go when Patsy gets back I shall return in time to get my help-group organised. By the way, I suppose there's no further news from the council about the school? Patsy handed in the petition with hundreds of names on it weeks ago.'

'No, my dear. Everything stops during the summer and you know what council and government departments are like. Next year will do for them, but come the autumn I'm sure the vicar will start worrying them. He's naturally eager to keep the youngsters in Kenelm.'

'I'm happy Cathy is going to support my help group.'

'Oh—that won't be possible, Fiona. That's what I wanted to tell you.'

His tone was almost joyous as if he was glad he'd just been reminded of his excuse for being here. 'Mrs Craven came to see me. She talked and talked, and I'm not betraying any confidences when I tell you that she and her husband have patched things up.'

'Patched things up?' Fiona exclaimed.

'Yes. She asked me to explain that Cathy has gone back to London to live with her father. They're hoping that he can help to get her in a college course for nursery nurses.'

'That'll be good, but the city won't be beneficial for Cathy's asthma.'

'It wasn't necessarily London's atmosphere that was entirely to blame for her condition. The reason they bought a house here was because Mr and Mrs Craven separated for a while. He, it seems, became rather too friendly with someone he worked with, and Mrs Craven being of a certain age and having menopause problems allowed their differences to escalate and grow out of all proportion. For Cathy's sake they tried to do things amicably, but she wasn't fooled. She blamed her mother for having to leave London, and in consequence she didn't do particularly well at school, and got in with bad company.'

'I thought there was *something*, and I'm glad it's been resolved. Let's hope it works out well for all of them. I shall hear probably from Anita. She's anxious to start another baby.'

James laughed. 'You aren't likely to be put out of business yet awhile.'

Fiona fell silent. She was being less than honest to talk of starting a help group for solvent users and drug addicts when all the time she was fighting a desire to move way from Kenelm.

'Will you marry me, Fiona?' James' words hung in the air, and in the growing dusk Fiona stared across the room at him, uncertain whether she had imagined his proposal.

'It's now or never, Fiona,' James said, not moving from the comfort of the easy chair. 'We've pussyfooted around long enough. If you say "yes" then we get married as quickly as possible.'

'James . . . I . . .' Fiona stood up, and James met her in the centre of the room.

'I lost you the day Stephen turned up, didn't I?' His voice was husky, an uncertain tremble evident, and Fiona experienced a heaviness of heart akin to a lead weight.

'James,' she said softly, 'I should have told you. Stephen and I knew one another a long time ago.'

'Why couldn't you have told me at the start? Why have you kept this a secret? You jilted Stephen for another doctor, not a nice thing to do, Fiona, but there must have been a good reason and it happens all the time. I am surprised at you, yes, even more surprised at your deceit.'

'I didn't intentionally deceive you, James. I tried to tell you that I knew Stephen, but you hurried on telling me all that you knew, enthusiastic about him coming into the practice, and it didn't seem the right time. How did you know anyway?'

'That Sunday afternoon when we were going to visit Dr Locke, Stephen asked me if it would make any difference to me knowing that you and he had once been engaged. It was a shock, but I guessed you must have your reasons for not telling me. I waited, hoping you would explain.'

'It was all a long time ago, James, and it's no good raking over old ashes.'

'But there is a spark still there, Fiona, so don't try to pretend.'

Fiona turned from him. 'If only he hadn't come back,' she said with genuine regret.

'You'd have married me while still loving another man?'

Tears began to prick her eyes. If only she could give James the full story, but how could she tell him that she would never ever stop loving Stephen? 'I'm very, very fond of you, James, and yes, if Stephen hadn't come here to remind me of the past I would have married you. Of course, you don't trust me now and I don't blame you, though the real truth isn't quite like Stephen sees it.'

'I still want to marry you, Fiona.'

She shook her head. 'No, James. I'm flattered that you should be so loyal, but things wouldn't be right.'

'Because you still want Stephen?'

'Stephen changed the course of his life. He went away embittered, but he found Martha who gave him three lovely children. He'll probably never marry again, so you see it will be better if when I go up to see my parents I get things sorted out in my mind, and if there are any jobs around I'll move away from Kenelm.' She faced James with tears trickling down her cheeks. 'The last thing I wanted was to hurt you, James, you've been such a wonderful friend.'

James sighed. 'That's what Laura keeps saying. Why can I never seem to find a woman who wants something more from me?'

'Perhaps you should look a little deeper into Laura's feelings for you. After the Abilenes' baby was born I had breakfast with Laura, and she told me all about Paul. It was only afterwards when I remembered the way she talked about you that I woke up to the fact that she loves you, James.'

'Laura? Loves *me*?' His expression changed from disbelief to renewed hope.

'You're right for each other,' Fiona said. 'Just as well we didn't rush into marriage, wasn't it?'

'I knew things weren't exactly right between us, there was always something holding you back, but I hoped it would resolve itself once we were actually living together. Fiona, don't move away from Kenelm. We can always be good friends. Just being able to talk like this means that we can be without involving emotions. I suppose that's what has always been missing.'

'During my holiday I'll try to decide to do what's best,' she promised.

A month later when Fiona returned from Selkirk she was no nearer to finding a solution. Jobs were harder to get in the north, and once she was back at work and discovered that James and Laura's friendship was rapidly developing, the need to move away seemed to diminish. She worked in harmony with all the doctors at the health centre, Stephen included, and he was a staunch supporter of the help group which commenced in the autumn. All the doctors, some retired ones as well as ministers of the local churches and professional people gave their time willingly to act as counsellors and the response from worried parents made the project well worth while.

The autumn days grew dark and chill, and as the winter gloom set in James and Laura announced that they were going into partnership together in the Midlands. Stephen took over as senior doctor at the health centre and Fiona worked with a will, grateful to occasionally see the man she loved even if he did seem to try to distance himself from her. She recognised that he had settled down to a comfortable life in the family home where security was all important to his children, and which gave him the opportunity to put all his energy into the work for which he was so well qualified.

He was on call one evening until midnight and after a full, heavy surgery he visited an elderly lady who had suffered a second stroke. He arranged the transfer from home to Gorton hospital, and personally took Mr Merridew back home after seeing his wife settled comfortably in a small one-bedded ward on the geriatric wing. He made tea for the old man and stayed to chat for over an hour until Mr Merridew's son arrived with his wife. Then Stephen went on to the health centre, and finding no further messages awaiting him he decided to sort out his case before going home when his spell of duty ended.

He went to file away Mrs Merridew's card after updating his report on her condition, and as his fingers went through the index which was in alphabetical order he stopped. FIONA MEREDITH. He continued slotting Mrs Merridew's card into the appropriate place then he went back, some strange curiosity driving him to pull out Fiona's card. He sat down at his desk intrigued by the lack of medical treatment until the years turned back one by one . . .

On the dot of midnight Stephen reported to the night emergency office that he was going off duty, but instead of turning towards Gorton he revved up his engine and headed for the rural caravan site. His mouth set hard, he vowed to himself that he didn't care whether Fiona was in bed or not, they had some straight talking to do, and he wanted a full explanation.

As he pulled up outside Fiona's mobile home he noticed that a light still burned in the lounge. He stretched across the flower-bed and tapped on the window, calling, 'Fiona, it's me, Stephen,' so as not to frighten her.

She peeped out, and Cassie barked, then she went to the door and opened it.

'Whatever's wrong?' she called. 'Is it Dr Locke?'

Stephen stalked angrily up the steps and into her sun-room. 'God, it's cold in here,' he said.

'It's warmer in the lounge, but why have you called this late?'

For several seconds—it seemed an age to Fiona—he stared at her, his dark eyes filled with recrimination.

'Stephen—for heaven's sake, whatever's the matter?'

'You're the matter,' he snapped back. 'You, your parents, Dr and Mrs Locke—Fiona, how could you treat me so badly?'

'I . . . I don't understand,' she stammered, pulling her warm dressing-gown more tightly round her.

'Oh, yes you do,' he growled impatiently. 'A crushed pelvis among your other injuries and you didn't tell me. *Me!* the man you were engaged to—*me*, the driver of the car you were in. God, woman, who were you trying to protect? I'm not stupid, I realise now the implications. Did you hate me so much that you couldn't even give me the chance to say I was sorry that you would never be able to have children? Was this other guy so much more sympathetic than I would have been?' He gripped her shoulders, shaking her violently as if in some way it made retribution for the past.

'Stop it!' Fiona yelled, fighting against his massive chest. 'You're hurting me, Stephen. Stop it!'

The glaze in Stephen's eyes cleared and he let Fiona go.

'Why? Why, Fiona? Why did everything change? —how could you stop loving me?'

Fiona buried her face in her hands and wept tears of relief.

'Can't you see?' she whispered eventually, 'it was because I loved you so much that I couldn't tie you to the promises we'd made, when I could no longer be a proper wife to you?'

He searched her face, his dark brown eyes softening with understanding, and then with a cry of anguish she fell into his outstretched arms.

'Oh, my darling, my darling,' he crooned, 'that you could love me *that* much. What must you think of me for throwing in the towel so easily, for—for pushing off and marrying someone else.'

'But that's what I wanted for you, Stephen,' she said.

'And I never blamed you for the accident. I believed that was fate.'

He pulled her against the warmth of his sheepskin coat and kissed her hair, her eyes, her lips with urgent passion.

'How can I ever repay your unselfishness? I'm not worthy of you—but oh, Fiona, if only you had told me, given me the chance to understand.'

'You would have married me out of pity,' she said. 'It would have been a barrier between us because you so desperately wanted a family.'

'And so did you—so you've been content to work among children, mums and babies. Oh, Fiona, my love, how cruel life has been to you.'

She shook her head. 'Not entirely,' she admitted. 'For a while I had James, but even he couldn't erase memories and then when you came back I realised with gratitude that you had found love, the proof of it in your family.'

'*Your* family too, my darling. It's what Martha wanted. I used her because I needed a woman and I used her badly sometimes because she wasn't you. Then one night when I'd had a bout of pneumonia all the misery and pain poured out. Martha helped me over that time and afterwards we settled for what we'd got. She was too good for me, a wonderful, gentle loving person and a splendid doctor. You'd have loved her and I hope you'll get to know her through our children. We aren't going to waste any more years are we, Fiona?'

She rested her head against his chest as tears of happiness fell unchecked.

'I was going to move away,' she said, 'but jobs aren't easy to find.'

'Then I'd have brought you back. You can't run out on

the people who need you, and I've just twisted Dad's arm into giving up that piece of land he owns near to the new church. We're going to have that new primary school, and we need you to fight for the government grant.'

'I've done with fighting,' she said.

'I'll do the fighting for you. If only you'd let me fight for you eleven years ago instead of you fighting against me. What a shocking waste it's all been.'

'No, darling,' she smiled up at him. 'You're fulfilled. All I wanted was your happiness.'

'And all I want is yours. The past is over—we'll start again, a little wiser, a little older, but with all the love in the world to give each other.'